WINNER OF THE PRESTIGIOUS
SEAL BOOKS FIRST NOVEL AWARD

JUDITH
by
Aritha van Herk

This extraordinarily moving story of one young woman's fight for self-sufficiency and love is the work of "a skillful writer . . . Her novel is as complex and rich as it can be . . . It is an impressive debut."

—Publishers Weekly

"Stark and stylistically memorable."

—Library Journal

"A lively piglet of a novel that will appeal to those who like their country matters raw and their pork larded with sexual politics."

—Times Literary Supplement

"A sensitive, warm, engaging story."

—Calgary Albertan

"This is a novel that reveals human experience with warmth and sensitivity. A brawling, passionate novel about hope, fears and courage."

—Ottawa Journal

"Remarkable and riveting."

—Montreal Gazette

Judith

Aritha van Herk

*This low-priced Bantam Book
has been completely reset in a type face
designed for easy reading, and was printed
from new plates. It contains the complete
text of the original hard-cover edition.*
NOT ONE WORD HAS BEEN OMITTED.

JUDITH
*A Bantam Book / published by arrangement with
McClelland and Stewart Limited*

PRINTING HISTORY
*Little, Brown and Company edition published October 1978
Book-of-the-Month Club Alternate March 1979
McClelland and Stewart edition published in Canada
October 1978
2nd printing .... November 1978
Book-of-the-Month Club edition December 1978
Bantam edition / September 1979*

*Photograph of author by
Rolf Kalman*

ISBN: 0-553-12384-X

Bantam Books are published by Bantam Books, Inc. Its trademark, consisting of the words "Bantam Books" and the portrayal of a bantam, is Registered in U.S. Patent and Trademark Office and in other countries. Marca Registrada. Bantam Books, Inc., 666 Fifth Avenue, New York, New York 10019.

PRINTED IN THE UNITED STATES OF AMERICA

This book is for Robert Jay, who believes.

"The time has come," the Walrus said,
"To talk of many things:
Of shoes—and ships—and sealing-wax—
Of cabbages—and kings—
And why the sea is boiling hot—
And whether pigs have wings."

Through the Looking Glass
LEWIS CARROLL

There is a herb in father's garden,
Some calls it maidens' rue:
When pigs they do fly like swallows in the sky,
Then the young men they'll prove true.

An old English folk song

One

Pig shit and wet greasy straw were piled high in the wheelbarrow. In the dim, dust-moted cavern of the barn, Judith slid the last forkful on top of the precarious heap and edged around the sow, stoic and braced in the middle of the pen. She climbed over the board fence into the aisle, the backs of her legs aching. Three pens and the goddamn wheelbarrow was full. Four pens and she lost half before she was out of the barn, had to pitch it back into the wheelbarrow again.

Left over from summer, cobwebs glimmered faintly in the low-ceilinged corners. The edges of the windows and the walls were blurred and indistinct; Judith squinted against the fine-particled haze. And underneath she felt the subterranean current of their breathing, the hot lift and fall of their shadowy ritual. She could hardly avoid it, sticky and resilient it caught at her the instant she dared to hesitate.

Walking down the aisle the length of the barn, she felt herself disjointed and awkward. Clumsily she heaved against the wind to shove open the back door. The fading daylight was a relief from the murky thickness inside. She thrust a stone against the door to hold it open, then listened for a moment to the wind wheeling around the break of poplars a hundred yards behind the barn.

Back inside, the cold followed. She bent to

the wheelbarrow and stood for a moment, leaning on her arms braced against the handles. The stiffness in her back and legs eased in the different posture but standing erect again it returned, a tight, cramping ache. Shouldering against the wind, she dumped the wheelbarrow over onto the growing pile of manure behind the barn, kicking out the last clump of dirty straw with her booted foot.

Darkness was easing down. Three pens left: one wheelbarrow full before she could slam the barn door and trudge up the hill to the house. She went back to shut the door against the cold and in the suddenly darker barn turned to find them all at attention watching her, a perfect succession of small eyes glowing like lantern pinpoints in the dusty light. With a motionless and uncanny intelligence they watched her, holding her captive. She felt her hands flat against the splintery wood of the door, hypnotized by their curiosity, the fathomless bottom of their knowing eyes.

Pigs. Ten sows. Ready to farrow in the next two months. Some of them maybe in three weeks. Gestation period for pigs: three months and three weeks and three days. She leaned her head back against the barn door and took a deep breath.

In the straw-muffled silence their bristling snouts and small orange eyes held her against the door. Dying light from the high, four-paned windows fell on their rough gray backs. The clean straw they had chewed into a nest in the corner of each pen was haloed with gauzy dust, and through that haze she saw them enchanted animals, Circe's humans standing fat-chinned in shafts of dusky light; like oracles.

So still and calm they were, so perfectly taut. And she was held there, could not will herself to move down the narrow aisle between their eyes.

She was held as immovable as she had been held under his eyes, his face crinkling into laughter. "You're a farm girl? You sure don't seem like a farm girl!"

Pigs. And more pigs. Soon there would be more, three months and three weeks and three days, and piglets and then weaners and then feeders and then market hogs, and she would have to buy a boar to cover all these sows again and . . .

"Shoo!" They jumped, startled at her shout and her waving arms, their cloven hooves scrambling across the straw-littered cement floor, whoofing and snorting.

"Damn you, damn you all anyway." She threw a chunk of the straw bale sitting at the far end of the barn into each of the last three pens. "You can rot in your own shit. I won't do any more tonight!" The startled sows eyed her from the backs of their pens, whoofing and grumbling their amazement. She banged the door shut behind her and pulled her body up the hill to the house.

After Daddy finished feeding the pigs, he would read to her.

"Are you done yet?" She raised her piping voice over the clatter of his feedpails.

"Pretty soon, Judy-girl. I just have to give the little ones water and then we're done and the pigs can go to sleep."

She waited for him outside, the darkness creeping in on the edges of the yard light. When he finally closed the barn door, she ran to catch his hand, taking two steps for his every one. His hand swallowed hers completely and in the twilight he loomed colossal beside her.

"If we went back, would they be sleeping already?" she asked.

"Maybe."

"Aren't they afraid of the dark?"

"Never."

After Judith was gone, they shifted restlessly, eyes gleaming in the straw-smelling darkness. Sniffing along the boards, they inhaled her resentment, snuffled at the mixed smell of her hatred and necessity. Still pondering, they stretched on their sides and extended their laden bellies on the straw to sleep calm and all-knowing.

Stiffness, it was locked in her bones, that insistent tension. At the house, she kicked off her rubber boots against the doorstep, then sat down on the narrow bench by the door to peel off the three pairs of socks she wore. Her feet seemed small and isolated after the bundling in the boots—too big for her. She had bought them in Macleods without trying them on, no longer thinking of her feet in terms of high-heeled platforms with dainty, narrow toes. She refused to think of that, denied it to herself. Oh well, they would be good for the winter; she could wear extra socks to keep warm and she wouldn't have to buy expensive lined boots. She would be working inside the barn anyway. They were clumsy but that was in its own way fitting, Judith no more those three-inch heels, the slight tapping on cement sidewalks, the rapping accompaniment on stairs, in the office hallway. Taking off her shoes in the afternoon to squirm her feet under the desk, hurriedly slipping them on again to go into his office to take a letter. Good feet, small and narrow, the arch emphasized by the height of the burnished leather and suede she always wore. Now they were helpless and out of place, uncalloused and resentful.

Barefoot first, she pulled off her jacket and sweater, undid the red kerchief binding her hair and ran her hand through it so that it stood on end, spiky, the ragged ends falling as close as a boy's. She felt again that lightness and the ebbing loss when she shook her head to find no weight at her neck.

Judith's long mocha hair lying in waves about the footrest of the dentist-like hairdresser's chair, the back of her neck feeling naked and vulnerable with its protection gone. She was almost giddy at first, she had been so long without a face, had always hidden it behind the frame of her hair. He would wrap it around his hand and tug at it, separating the tendrils with his fingers and twisting it until she shook her head with annoyance. And he laughed, holding her like that, captive.

After the whispering barn, the yellow-painted kitchen was still and hollow, not even the ticking of a clock to fill the silence that domestic noises could not shut out. Before going to the barn, she would turn on the light in the house to ease the darkness waiting when she came in. From the barn, the kitchen window that looked across the yard shone with a kind of steadfastness, a goal to be reached when all the chores were done. Always that connection between the kitchen window and the barn, across the expanse of yard.

At the window Judy peered through cupped hands into the darkness. "When is Daddy coming?"

Her mother stood in front of the stove. "Is the light in the barn still on?"

"Yes."

Cold glass against her nose, Judy watched until the barn light snapped into darkness. "He's coming. The light's off."

"Set the table then, Judy."

Judith did not bother to set herself a plate but rummaged in the cupboard for crackers and cheese. Sitting sideways at the old drop-leaf table, she ate listlessly, looking out at the now-dark yard.

Down the hill the barn was a silent, contained red shadow. It held an existence entirely without her, shielding those secretive creatures inside.

At her bare, too-small desk—knees banging the top—she opened the account book. Every quarter, every penny—$5.99 for each infrared heat lamp, $3.29 for a tooth clipper, $558 for lawyer's fees. Straw bales—$425. Ten sows at $200 each—$2,000. God. And it would be so long, having to feed them and herself all winter, before any of them could be sold. She didn't want to touch the rest of the inheritance—that was to pay off the land. Unless she could sell some weaners. But no, her father used to say, "You lose money selling weaners, you have to sell market hogs, feeders."

She looked at the calendar above the desk. Eight months at least before she could know if it would even work. And what if they got sick? It recurred and recurred, the same idea. Failure.

She flipped the stiff black cover of the account book shut, refused to look at it anymore. At the bathroom sink she splashed her face before dropping her clothes on the floor and sliding naked into the narrow bed in her room at the back of the house. Her room. The rest of the house was separate and with no knowledge of her; it sided with the barn. She had sold her four-poster brass bed, knew it to be an encumbrance, an archive of her nights in the city, the difficulty her other self had getting up from it to take the bus to the office every morning.

In the morning the tension would still be there, settled in her frame. Going to bed at ten, exhausted from shoveling shit, climbing fences, pushing straw bales, carrying feed or water pails

—full or empty, they were a pressure on her aching arms. Setting her alarm for six but unable to drag herself out of her lethargic nest in the hard, narrow bed. She lay on her stomach and would not get up.

He would run his hand down the length of her back, smoothing her buttocks, caressing the backs of her knees. "Always lying on your stomach. Like a baby," he said, even as she moved impatiently, restless under his touch, angry with his assumption of her body. But still savored it, the captivity.

And now she could not rouse herself against the morning, but burrowed deeper into the unyielding bed and refused to think of them waiting in the barn, morning light on their pale backs. Finally at eight she made herself emerge, stiff with sleep and resentment. Every day carried a tedium she felt in her very bones as she struggled into blue jeans and a sweater.

For Judith it had been the lethargy of city, having to force herself over the side of the high brass bed and fumble her way into the morning, always racing to catch the bus with her scarf untied and her coat open. Then, had to go into the office washroom to brush her hair, unscramble the knots that sleep had left.

Standing at the kitchen window she looked out at the farmyard, the barn and the two empty granaries, gray and unpainted. The previous owner had harvested the fall crop before she came and before she had formal title to the land. Already it was November; the yard would ring dully with the frost in the ground on her way to the barn. There was no snow yet but everything seemed brittle and resounding. She hunched her shoulders under the sweater. Not to have to go out there, the barn thick and steamy after the night; the pigs rousing and their bodies churning up their earthy smell. To the south her thin driveway threaded its way between a line of evergreens to the road. Snow would catch between the trees and it would be hell to get out in the winter; she'd have to have it cleared.

"Just a minute," she said aloud, pulling on her boots against the cramp of her muscles. "There's no snow yet. Think about that when you have to. Only when you have to . . ." But walking to the barn, she turned to look at the driveway again.

"You don't wanna plant trees along the drive. They catch the snow and it's impossible to get out after a blizzard," her father had said to her mother. In the glassy November mornings before school, Judy rode her bike, bouncing over the frozen ruts and almost ringing in the cold, her hair streaming as she pedaled furiously, laughing, to the end of the driveway and back again and again breathless in the morning until she had to stop and go in for breakfast.

"I wish it wouldn't snow, then I can ride my bike forever."

"Don't think about winter until it comes, Judy-girl. It'll be here before you know it."

Going down the hill to the barn she felt herself walking the way city women walk, as if stepping over cracked eggs. She had to remind herself that there was no one to watch her, no one. It mattered not a damn if she was clumsy. Just the pigs, she told herself, just the pigs. Think of them, think of next spring.

She knew they would be waiting, that row of massive heads over the boards. She knew that the minute she opened the barn door they would shuffle to their feet; the minute they heard her clanking buckets and five-gallon pails they would begin to sniff and snort. Laboring over the pails, she worked silently, measured the feed exactly, a pail of water for each sow.

They waited at their fences, unafraid but distant, watching her always. Even with their feed in the trough they waited, refusing to eat in front of her, waiting for her to leave them alone. And she would not confront their awareness directly but moved between the pens in a circle of isolation, feeding them and ignoring them in a silence of her own. They waited, patronizing, small eyes and bristling snouts following her movements.

They're only pigs, she insisted to herself. And hurried through her contact with them, left the barn with relief to work in the yard, fixing fences and clearing up the lumber left scattered about.

They ate then, munching quietly in the opaque breath of the barn, cleaning their troughs with energy. Still restless in their new surroundings, they waited without anxiety for her to return, watched for more of her abrupt movement. Three weeks they had been here and still she edged them, surrounded them with her careful distance.

Working in the yard, she wished for the next six months of days to vanish, for spring to leave behind the interminable winter between her and the sows. She turned it over and over in her mind as if it were a coin she handled: Would they work. Would she work?

Hands and thoughts separate, she smeared putty around the cracks of the barn windows to prevent the wind from creeping in; even working from the outside she could feel their snuffling through the walls. Only ten sows, but their very body heat penetrated. It was a constant reminder, and while she struggled to ignore them she was always conscious of their presence, alive and musky.

Every day was getting colder, the air more brittle. In the morning a thin scab of ice rested on the puddles of water. Warming with the work outside, she felt her body ease and release some of its stiffness.

In the lithe energy of her childhood, she remembered dancing, hopping, skipping, mother and father on either side, a hand in each of theirs and her small body like a charged wire, feeling the strength in herself flowing from them. She was the vibration between their steadier feet, their joining.

He must have been watching her for five minutes, the tall, lanky man in the checkered jacket. She was hammering at a sagging rail of the fence beside the barn. When the market hogs had to be shipped next summer, she would need a loading pen, but she could hammer now in the November mornings with the bleak sun almost warm on the top of her head.

When she lifted her eyes to meet his, the first thought that came to her was, God, I've been here for three weeks without seeing a soul. I haven't left this place for three weeks. And she wondered how she had managed, whether she hadn't needed butter and milk, then realized that she had been living out of cans and boxes.

The red-faced man in the duck-billed hat nodded politely. "Didn't think there was anyone here yet. I got the place two miles down the road and we've been wondering when you all would move in."

"How are you?" She put her bruised hands in her pockets quickly, thinking, I will not shake hands, I will not. "I'm Judith Pierce."

He stood looking about the yard. Finally his eyes came back to her, standing with her hands muffled in her pockets. "Looks like you've been working pretty hard here."

She looked around her too, suddenly surprised. The handle of the barn door was fixed, the cracks around the windows were filled, she had cleared dead weeds from against the side of the barn, the fence beside her no longer leaned. "Oh," she said hesitantly. "Well, there's lots to do."

"Yeah, always plenty to do on a farm." He studied her for a moment. Under his eyes she felt that she was small and slight, ineffectual. "Hope you like living here," he said easily. "People are real friendly." He looked up at the sky. "Anything I can help you with?"

"No. No, I don't think so," she said quickly, angry at herself for being five-foot-five, for the ridiculously large boots on her feet. "Nothing."

He looked at her again for a long moment, then down at the ground. "You all alone?"

"Yes."

"Husband not here yet? Still works in the city?"

"No. I'm not married."

He crinkled his eyes and waited.

"I'm here alone." She was suddenly angry at herself for being alone, for explaining to this man. Who the hell was he? Wouldn't even say his name. She turned away, rigid, refusing to look at him.

"Kinda funny thing for a girl to do alone," he said, lifting his hat to scratch his head. "Hell, I got three boys and I can hardly keep up on my place. What you got here?"

"Farrowing sows," she said shortly, even glaring at him.

He nodded. "Ever done it before? Little thing like you be worn out in two months."

"I've done it before," she said stiffly, "and it's going fine." Her fists clenched inside her pockets.

"Sure." He was suddenly agreeing with her. "Was this barn ready for sows?"

"No, I hired a carpenter." Gripping the fence post, she found her hand out of her pocket, dirt grimed in her knuckles and her nails ragged and broken.

"What are you feeding them?"

"Barley, soymeal, minerals. They're doing all right."

"You know anything about baby piglets? What if they get sick?"

"They won't," she said furiously, spitting the words between her teeth, "because I am not going to allow any farmers to walk in this barn and give my pigs their diseases. My father never let anybody in his pig barn."

"You grew up on the farm then?"

"Yes, my father was a farmer. The best around."

"What did you say your name was?"

"Pierce."

"Oh yeah, big pig farmer in Stettler county five years ago." He hesitated. "But he sold out."

"Yes." She looked down at the ground.

"Should've taken over his farm." She said nothing. "Well," quickly, "you can probably handle a few pigs. Least you seem to know a little about it. Just hope the price doesn't go down. Sure I can't help you with anything now?"

"No," she said. "I'm fine." Useless, her anger started to dissolve and she felt her body weak and relaxed on the heels of its tension.

"Well, come on over some night. My wife would be glad to have you for supper. Name's Ed Stamby." He turned to go. "And if you ever need any help just holler. Don't suppose you'll want to do any castrating or tailclipping by yourself."

"Thanks," she said quietly. "I'll let you know. Nice of you to come over."

She stood watching the blue pickup truck go down the lane. Suddenly wakened out of her dreamy state, she speculated: I'd better go to town and get some groceries and maybe I'd better trade in the car for a half-ton.

Two

Inside the barn the landscape diminished into background. Here everything was greater than reality, boundaries undefined. It was their gray-blue aura, an insular warren; they made it so, the palpable illumination in the cave-like barn was their own.

Awake, their red eyes shone like insect beacons through the humming tumescence of their territory. In their own steamy rotundity their wariness receded; still they pondered the almost-familiar barn, searching for indicators she could have left, signs for them to snuff up. The board fences that separated them were warm and new, and sun-cured straw lay thick on the cement floor. They itched their backs and rumbled in their folding throats with pleasure. Comfort was all very well but it lacked salt with her so stiff and edgy she refused to dance for them, so deadly and killingly serious that they edged back from her, disgruntled.

They had come a long journey, feeling the wind lean against the truck box in that violent hurtling pen, their unease making them stand rigid and upright the length of the ride, shifting with the movement that carried them. They pressed their flat snouts against the slatted sides of the truck box and gleamed at the trees and miles of fences whipping by. They knew trees and fences, remembered them from some hollow background of youth before they were enclosed in concrete and metal among hundreds of others so much like them; the same mealy chop and iron-tinged water for all, and only the man human, a dim form walking down the dividing aisle between the cold aluminum mesh of the pens. Always there, they accepted him and ignored him, just as they knew him well, his acrid maleness overwhelming the smell of old chop dust in his coat. Chopped nutty oats dropped into the troughs every four hours and the shit disappeared through the slatted floor at the end of the pen. There was no yellow-warm straw, only cement, cool and neutral.

They had toted up their own completeness and perfection. In the truck they were divided from the ordinary bunch and put in a small, tight pen by themselves. The movable gates were deceptive but comforting, separating their shiny, well-fed whiteness and quickening pregnancy from the splotched and muddy tangle of hooves and floppy ears on the other side of the gate sectioning the truck box.

Unlike the other bunch, they refused to fight. The familiar smell they found on each other huddled them together; they pressed their flat and well-formed noses against the slats of the truck gates with dignity. Decorously preoccupied with the countryside, they ignored the alien grunts and squeals from the other side of the partition that accompanied them the length of the journey. Aloof and singled out, they knew this was portentous.

And she was there at the end of the journey. Even the damp, clinging smell of concrete and strange people could not hide that this one was she. Unlike the other human—the man already forgotten—they remembered her distinctly; her voice, her motions, her faintly grassy smell. Remembered her standing in the aisle of the barn in a chop-colored coat, her hair long and burnished under the naked 60-watt lightbulbs. Pointing at them with a short stick, laughing and exhilarated. "That one, and that one . . . she looks nice!"

Portentous, they knew it, they remembered and felt themselves chosen. The man inside the pen with them nodded, the scrape of the red, waxy-smelling livestock marker over their backs. Even his vinegary overalls brushing against them could not overcome the female scent she threw. When she had pointed out ten, she clapped her hands and laughed again, her pale face alight.

The man stood in the middle of their pen, scratching his own huge bristly ear, sardonic and unamused. "They're two hundred apiece," he said. She nodded yes but disregarded him completely, had eyes only for them—her plump white sows with thickening bellies and tight young tits.

She was waiting. They sensed it, skittering nervously off the truck and down the slatted chute. Balking and hesitant, they edged warily forward into the cavernous barn, squealing a little as she and the trucker slapped and prodded them into separate pens—board fences between each one of them. Anxious, they gnawed and chaffed at the boards but subsided finally to the straw and warmth. Watchful, they were yet unafraid. The enclosing barn was an extension of her; she pervaded the sweet, fir-tinged dust in the air.

After the strangeness of the new place disappeared and when she was not there, they grunted and moaned with pleasure. Rubbing their itchy backs against the rough new wood, rooting deep into the thickness of crackling straw; she could not apprehend the sense of herself that they snuffed up, that they overtook and claimed. They reserved their wariness for her presence, waiting for her voice and her laughter, waiting for her tightness to slip and for her to reveal herself and let their common female scents mingle. Her smell was the same as they remembered but there was an edge of bitterness to it, a tinge of anxiety. And she was not exhilarated but fierce and distant, as rigid and brittle as if she were hedging herself against them, as if she were afraid now that she had chosen them.

It was unreal to her until the sows arrived. They pinned her down, leaving no way out. When the truck backed up to the barn door and the trucker prodded them down the narrow chute, she wanted to run—God, they were huge, they were stubborn, how would she ever handle them! How could she do it? They were used to slats and cement and a feed and water system, not wooden pens and a person cleaning them out every day. And they were all young, had never farrowed before. What if they turned on her, refused to let her near and crazily crushed their piglets, her precious investment?

"Why are we getting more pigs, Daddy? Don't we have enough?" She swung her body back and forth between her hands and feet, clinging to the rails of the chute. She could feel her pigtails flopping up and down on her back.

He closed the gate and came around the chute to lift her to the ground. "It's an investment."

"What's an 'vestment?"

He laughed. "Buying something so that you'll get more back, Judy-girl."

Pigs make more, she thought, and more pigs. Funny.

The trucker helped her separate them into individual pens, his cowboy boots impatient and efficient. They were uneasy but docile. She sighed and zipped up her jacket when they were all installed and separate, one by one was safer than the bunch of them, a mass of bristly backs and glowing eyes, the force of them against her impossible to withstand.

"Okay," she said a little too loudly. "I guess that's it."

"Nice bunch of sows." His dark eyes narrowed as he pushed back his cowboy hat to scratch greasy hair.

"Yes," she said, hesitating only a little.

"Goin' into business?" He was interested, amused at the doubt that showed on her face.

She only looked at him. "Come into the house and I'll pay you."

He drove the few hundred yards to the house, braked the truck and jumped out with a bravado that only crossed her mind obliquely as she went ahead of him into the little porch. She was thinking of the pigs, the pigs; they were in the barn now, she would have to go out and feed and water them. Alone. She wanted to postpone it forever, wanted the driver to go back out with her, his easy cowboy boots to muffle their animal superiority.

Sitting sideways at the kitchen table, he filled out the bill. "There you are . . . hope it's okay."

She glanced at it quickly, not seeing the calculation. Wrote a check for the total in her tight hand and signed it carefully, Judith Pierce, with no flourishes.

She had signed everything for him so carefully, her hand as restrained and uninvolved as it should be signing his letters, his memoranda. Controlled, picking up the receiver and speaking without a tremor, slitting open the mail, typing business letters, her careful fingers creating the words at a touch of the keys. The door closed, he reached out to touch her hand on the just-dictated letter and she retreated, angry at his intrusion on her control, fingers only wanton after five, only then letting them touch his clean jaw, the chest beneath the striped silk tie.

"Pierce," the trucker said. "Pierce. That sounds familiar."

"Yes." Unnecessarily, "That's my name."

"And you're startin' up farming."

She nodded, hands before her restless on the table.

He shook his head. "Don't know how you can do it. Price of things these days. I had a farm but I couldn't do it. It's a heck of a lot better truckin' livestock and feed for farmers than bein' one yourself."

She took a long, quiet breath. It was too late. They were there now.

He raised dark eyebrows at her over inquisitive eyes. "I'd say you were a city kid. What d'ya figure, you're gonna come out here and lead an easy life?"

She shook her head. "No."

"Got a little money, figured you may as well buy a piece of land." He chuckled disgruntledly. "Sold my farm to a city fella. It's some kind of new deal for people with money. You sure can't farm without money."

"I know."

"Hey, maybe you wanna find a nice farm boy? I could send a couple your way."

She shook her head again.

He waited a moment, then shrugged. "Not my business."

She looked at him then. "You're right, it's risky."

He stared her up and down, eyes unrelenting. "You're not very old. Musta had a pretty good job if you can buy a farm. Now if I had a nice city job, I wouldn't give it up for nothin'."

Someone else's blood, it's all built on someone else's blood. "I was just a secretary," she said, but he was at the door, settling the dirty cowboy hat on his head with a twitch.

"Good luck. Need a trucker, give me a call. I'm always shipping into the city. Can bring back almost anything you need."

"Thanks. I guess I'll need some more feed in about a month."

"Sure, just call me. Wife takes all the calls. She'll write it down. Number's on the bill."

"Okay, thanks."

She watched the red two-ton truck drive down her tree-lined lane, branches bare against the bright sky. "You never asked," she said aloud, her eyes following the truck as it turned onto the main road, "but I was a secretary." She repeated it to herself. "A secretary."

Judith Pierce. Occupation: administrative secretary. Gross salary: $9,039 per year. Description of duties: general clerical and secretarial duties for supervisor as well as responsibility in compiling reports, dealing with supervisor's overflow.

"Would you mind finishing these up before you leave tonight, Judith?"

She reached for the stack of files, his fingers sliding over hers as he handed them to her. Surprised, she looked up to his deliberate eyes on her face. And an hour later, the office deserted, was less surprised to feel those same cool, narrow fingers on the back of her neck, lifting her hair and turning her face upwards.

They were out in the barn, the pigs. Hers now, the check already deducted from her bank balance. She had paid the breeder when she picked them out. And now she would have to stay. The last five days that she had spent here alone and wandering about the fields were nothing but play.

"Daddy, where are you? Wait for me." The

wind lifted her hair, flung itself against her body. She ran and ran into the wind. It swallowed her words and left them soundless; she feel to her knees, sobbing for breath, and staggered up again. The field was so big; she had been running forever. And then from the top of the pasture hill she saw him below, her father striding the dusty path home, the pig walking sedately in front of him. Between the scissored movement of his blue-overalled legs flashed the sow's swaying lard behind, tail curled over her lifted pink sex as she tripped back to the escaped pen.

Everything began with them; she had only been waiting for them to arrive to set everything in motion and make it real. Now. She began rushing about aimlessly, hunting for a sweater and jacket. What if they had crashed over the low board fences and were rooting up the barn with their furious wrinkled snouts? She dug frantically for old socks and boots through suitcases and boxes still half-packed, scattered through the house from kitchen to bedroom. God, no boots! She cursed herself. In all her planning, feed pails and water pails, chop and pitchforks and shovels, she had forgotten to buy rubber boots. She clawed through a box of shoes in search of her winter boots, then held them at arm's length in disgust. High-heeled, fashionable suede leather cossack boots. She threw them back in the box and pulled out a pair of low shoes. Sitting on the bench by the door she fumbled with the laces, her fingers trembling with haste. And then could not bring herself to move; sat there, unwilling and afraid.

She knew they would be waiting for her. She knew they would be watching, wondering at her, that her every move would occupy them. She was their stranger and she must reconcile them. They would accept nothing less. And she was dependent on them.

She stood and put her hand on the coolness of the doorknob. Come on, she thought, come on. Where's your guts? Isn't this what you waited for? Isn't this what you planned? Isn't this what you worked for?

She twisted the knob and pulled the door open, walked down the hill like a lagging marionette, looking at bare branches against a cold sky with her hands thrust deep into her blue jean pockets. She wished intensely for the truck driver's loud cheerfulness, even disparagement. What in God's name was she doing with sows? It had been so easy, every day the electric gray keys singing under her fingers, every day the routine; eight-thirty to pull the cover off the typewriter, ten to take his cup to the sink and wash it, fill it with coffee and bring it to him. Twelve for lunch. Back at one, the afternoon folding into the morning with the paper and the last of the day's new letters. Three, his coffee again, and five, flicking the switch on the machine, slipping the cover over its face like reassuring a child for the next day. She counted the days on her fingers, slipping them off like beads for a whole year, and in the end checking the very hours off on her calendar, moving through them like a specially choreographed dance only for her, in perfect step with the rest of them; but because she was slicing the days off, her dance was not interminable. That was her secret and her refuge.

And now you're afraid, she reprimanded herself at the bottom of the hill, of a little bunch of pigs that belong to you and that you can do what you want with. Or at least try to, she corrected herself, the stored-up confidence of a year ebbing away.

"I didn't think it would be like this," she

said aloud. "I thought it would be easy." As easy as with him, tagging behind him, beside him, her small fist on the handle of the pail close to his reddened and rough one. The big hand that set the pail down to squeeze hers, that picked her up and swung her over the fences too high for her climb.

"Wait here, Judy-girl." She perched, a queen on the top rail, while he shoveled feed and called them, then fought his way back to her through a milling press of roughened bristly backs and snorting snouts chomping with gusto.

He put her outside at the door when he separated sows that were due to come in. "When I say, you open it," he told her. She stood, tense and ready, her hand tight on the handle, so eager to please him. "Okay," he shouted, "open it." Miraculously the right sow appeared and they herded it to the other barn, Judy running to keep up with him and the heavy, swaying sow.

And later she watched the pigs for him, their appetites and vigor; running into the house: "Dad, there's a sick pig in the feeder barn. You better give him some penicillin, right?"

And he was always there for her to run to, always there with his hands and his arms and his rough-grained voice.

Judith hesitated in front of the barn's new door. She had never before done anything without him and still she wondered, as she had wondered on that hot September Saturday two months ago, leaning on the edge of the sawhorse and watching the gray-whiskered carpenter planing the edges of the new door, if it could be possible without him.

The carpenter had worked so slowly that she was bored and impatient, wanting the old barn to be done in a day: neatly divided into pens, boards fitting the slots, everything measured and square. He worked deliberately all August and September; she knew that it would take that long, but wanted him to hurry, hurry.

He had been the only one who answered her advertisement in the local newspaper. Apprehensive that he would be expensive and crotchety, she drove down from the city one weekend to talk to him. She knocked on his door at noon, hoping he would be home for dinner. And knew him the minute he came to the door, rubbing his chin, the corners of his mouth faintly black. She looked at him blankly, the years sliding away in front of her.

"Yes?" he asked.

"I put the ad in the paper," she said. "You answered my letter."

"The name kind of struck me. Been a few years, but I figured it might be you."

"Yes," she said, bewildered. "I didn't remember your name, but I do now."

"C'mon in." She followed him into the small, disorderly kitchen—his wife must have died—and edged herself down on one of the wooden chairs. "You buildin' on your dad's farm?"

"No, it's sold."

"Yup, I knew that. Figured you might have bought it back."

"No," she said, twisting her fingers together. She stared at the round patterns of the linoleum, unwilling to look at him. Seeing instead all the afternoons in the sun under the shadow marks of the new rafters, the roof not on yet and the cement clean and gray. Judy bringing the pitcher of lemonade, having to carry it so heavy; handing nails to her father up the ladder, climbing on the unshingled roof, knees skinned and arms black with sun and dirt. When Judy's mother went to town, she asked him if he wanted anything and his answer was always the same. "Can you bring me some more snoose?" dipping his hand into his pocket. Her mother took the money, Judy dancing around her, waiting to go along in the car to town, to the post office, the store, more nails and more snoose.

"Too bad," the old carpenter said, "to let it go." He raised thick and graying eyebrows at her. "Sure was a nice place, your father's, specially after we finished that new barn."

"I couldn't buy it back." She shifted nervously on the hard chair and cleared her throat, fighting angry tears. "Can you do some work for me then?" and her voice was harsh. "Or don't you have time?"

"Well, I don't do much carpenter work now, too old and the wife just died a few years back, but if you want me I could do a little. What you planning on?"

"I bought Johnson's eighty over by the correction line. I want to change the barn for sows and fix up the house a little."

He looked at her. "You were working in the city."

"Yeah, it wasn't so good."

"Well, your dad didn't much want to sell that farm."

She looked again at the circles on the linoleum floor. Patterns of circles of circles. "Will you do it?"

"Don't you want to know how much?"

"How much?"

"Six dollars an hour."

She shrugged. "Sure." She wished that he was someone else, someone strange, but there could be no one else.

Her father had leaned against the tractor wheel. "Sure, six days a week and $2.00 an hour." His face hung in mournful folds, he was shriveled beside the stocky bulk of her father. But stringy and resilient. The barn rose in weeks, cement foundation, two-by-four shell, plywood sides, rafters; every day a transformation.

"Shall I clean the sow pens, Daddy? Then you can finish the shingles."

"Don't you want to wait for me?"

In the sow barn, secret and alone, her legs barely reaching over the pens, scraping the shovel over the cement floor and lifting it to the wheelbarrow. So heavy, her arms lifting and shoving, lifting and shoving, back and forth the length of each pen in the rich dimness, with rotund sows and piglets rustling around her until the door burst open with his feed pails. "You're working in the dark, Judy, you forgot to turn the light on." The enclosed pig world widening to take him in, always the center, around it the circle.

"Okay," the carpenter said. "When do you want me to start?"

"If you want you can come over this afternoon and I'll show you what I want done in the barn and the house. I can't stay out there until the house is fixed up. And I can't do anything until the barn is ready, so I want it done as quick as possible."

"Sure," he said and he smiled for the first time, returning to her a memory of his stained and broken teeth. "I'll just come along with you now, nothing better to do." And he shuffled his body into his coat.

He had worked all August and September, refusing to be hurried, but doing it exactly to her specifications. Hammered and sawed in silence, spitting the snuff she still brought him from Norberg to strike the earth outside the barn.

She would drive out to the farm only on

Saturdays, used the excuse that she was shopping downtown, then headed the car out of the city. During the week she worked absently, and lagged all day Sunday, exhausted with the frantic effort of transition. Those Saturdays she worked with the old man in the barn, silently; he talked little, measuring and hammering, the whir of his electric saw intermittent with the late pulsating summer.

The barn was almost finished and the row of pens on either side of the center aisle gleamed white wood; he was putting on the new door, planing it to perfection. He put down the chisel and, selecting neatly, stuffed a thick black wad into his cheek. They had talked only of the weather and baseball but now he seemed to want to plunge into something else.

"This is gonna cost you a fair bit," he said suddenly, not looking at her. "An eighty, getting this barn fixed up, gonna have to put critters in these pens, buy straw . . . Good thing you don't have to put in water or electricity."

"I know," she said. "I know that."

"So, you're spendin' what's left of your dad's farm on this."

"Well, I've been saving my money for years."

"Sure. But I don't suppose a secr'tary could save enough to buy a farm. Even an eighty's pretty expensive now."

"What should I have done with his money? Gone to Hawaii like every other city slicker?" You don't know, she thought. It's all I've got left of him, it's all that's left of anything. And he knew, oh he knew. I couldn't touch it until I was twenty-one and by then I'd finally realized. And now I know for sure and this is it, this is my last chance. If I don't do it now I never will and I'll never do anything at all, and I'll never please him.

He stared at her in astonishment as she left the barn and drove away, the small red car speeding over the dusty road. Working late, he finished the barn that night and moved the saw-horse and the electric saw to the house. Both of them ignored the conversation the next Saturday, Judith happy to pretend it had never taken place.

There was not so much to be done in the house; it had at least been boarded up against the wind and the open spaces. She visited the breeder and told him she would send a truck for the newly bred sows in two weeks.

And then the final transition, her last day at the office. The other girls had bought her a rose and pinned it on her dress, joking about the job she was getting, such a good job she wouldn't even tell them about it. She thanked them, nervous and fidgety, said that she might be back; but they waved her away, already blocking her out of the symmetrical choreography, already another girl, bangs and blonde hair, trained to take her place; memorize the filing system, type the memos, slit open the morning's mail.

He waited until the end of the day before he called her into his office. Closing the door firmly, he put his arm around her with more gentleness than she could remember. "Look, Judith, be reasonable. Won't you change your mind? It's not too late."

She shook her head, silent.

He walked to the window and stood looking out, then turned back to her again. "I still don't understand why you want to quit this job."

Judith sat down and turned her hands over in her lap. "I already have," she said mildly. The black dress emphasized her palenes. The Saturdays at the farm when he thought she was shopping were not visible except for a faint glimmer in her hair. "Isn't there reason enough?"

"I know, but we've managed so far. That shouldn't matter at this point."

Judith shrugged. "It's still not very good. My conscience bothers me."

"Okay, but I just don't understand why it took you this long to decide that. Besides, you haven't even got another job yet. You could at least let me help you find one. I think something else's bugging you."

She watched him fingering the double knot of his expensive tie, brown hand against his throat a reminder, those adept brown fingers. "I'll tell you about everything on Sunday night," she said.

"Well, if that's the way you want it. Why can't you tell me now?"

"Please," she said. "Please."

"All right, all right. I'll come over on Sunday. I'd come on Saturday, but I have to go to this stock club deal."

"Okay," she said softly, rising.

"Are you sure you're not mad at me for doing something drastically wrong?"

She shook her head, hair falling lightly about her shoulders. In the elevator on the way down she clutched the handrail, looking steadily before her and trying to think of her field, her barn. They were hers, a place for her to go. Moving swiftly down the street then, she turned into a low building and went down a flight of stairs into the smell of soap and hair spray, of bleaching agent. "Cut it," she said to the hairdresser, lifting her hair with her hands. "All off."

She'd rented a truck and hired a couple of men to load the furniture for her, driven to a used-furniture store and sold what she didn't want, then drove the truck out to the farm. Unloading was awkward but not impossible; her furniture was light and spindly. She cursed and staggered but somehow edged it off the truck and pushed and shoved it through the door into the house. The next day she drove the truck back, cleaned the apartment and handed in her keys.

"No forwarding address," she told the caretaker. "I'm going to be traveling for a while."

"But what about your mail? What about your damage deposit?"

"I don't know where I'll be, you see," she said lamely. "None of the mail will be important. Wait—you can send it to my lawyer." She scribbled down the address.

She thought of him going to the apartment on Sunday, fitting his key into the lock and swinging open the door on the empty walls, as still and unbreathing as if no one had ever lived there.

> This will be a surprise to you, but I'm moving away/you haven't done anything wrong, though. Sorry I couldn't tell you this before, but my secrets always work best. If you want my car back get in touch with my lawyer.
> Love/Judith.

She knew he wouldn't want the car back, would be furious and icy and coiled, but after a week would slip into another woman, the new secretary perhaps.

She reached out to grasp the handle of the barn door, turned it and went in. They were all standing at attention anticipating her arrival, the row of mammoth heads exactly the same turn and inclination. They re-examined her differentness, her ears now as available as their own. They liked that, the cleanness of her face without her hair. But she was rigid and brittle; she refused to speak to them even though the bravest of them whoofed softly to encourage her. The rest waited, reserved.

She clanked her pails loudly as if she wanted to sing to herself but could not. They heard water rushing into a pail through the chorehouse partition and then her movement. She banged a full pail down in the aisle and started measuring feed into troughs. Backed into the furthest corner of the pen while she scooped it out for them, their wariness gave them an oblique and distanced view of her as she leaned over each fence. She was flushed, knew herself to be at a disadvantage but they would not move closer, conscious of her fear and her wish for distance. Tight and drawn, she fed and watered them quickly, awkwardly; they could not object to that, they felt for her awkwardness, had liked it when she chose them, standing in the middle of their old barn. But she was hurried and jerky and she left them too quickly, sure of their comfort and safety but not lingering over them. Restrained, they snuffed about their pens, did not approach their troughs until the door closed behind her. Then they moved forward carefully, sniffed, tasted and munched quickly and with no enjoyment, only the necessity of hunger.

Uneasy but patient they waited. Day after day they edged around her, as carefully as she edged them. She seemed only to grow stiffer, more rigid and unyielding to the proximity of their hides. She carried a smell of anger with her like a stick, as if she had been tricked; they retreated before it. Waiting always, they paced their individual pens, looking over the fences at each other with soft grunts. They moved in a silence with her; she never spoke to them, reserving her words to herself.

More familiar with their surroundings and less restless every day, they paced the necessities of their ordered days: sleep, food, arranging the nest, feeling the movement in their bellies. And with the stubbornness of piggy patience, determined to outwait her.

Three

In the morning she flung the door open with a new energy. She measured feed and poured water into their troughs as silently and scrupulously as before, but now her visible momentum made her less remote; they felt her bending toward them. Moving to their troughs, they bent their heads one by one and dipped snouts into their brown mash. She stood completely still. They had never eaten in front of her before, had waited until the door shut behind her to swallow and munch surreptitiously, her only knowledge of their appetite the empty troughs.

Her small hands clutching at the fence, she stood on tiptoe to see over it. "They eat so fast."

"No, Judy, it only looks that way. They sort of talk by munching, so they're doing more than eating."

She pressed her hand against his overalled leg, so solid and rough.

"Who do they talk to?"

"Each other of course."

Broad backs visible above the fence, they ducked heads down to their feed. She moved again, seeming to ignore them. They swung their heads back and forth, comparing with loud smacks, then thrust them down for another mouthful and up again to snort and swallow. It had a rhythm of its own, their eating; balanced and fine, the timing important. She played a part yet remained separate, the careful ripples of her bone and muscle as she moved quietly back and forth: threw a packet of straw into the back of each pen, hammered tight a loose nail by the door. Through the dust that rose from the straw they sensed her response; she was moving her ragged head, her hands with them! Those narrow white hands with jagged nails and battered knuckles straining at the handles of feed pails, grasping the shovel and pitchfork, antagonistic. So defenseless and weak while attacking so much.

In that other barn, the man's barn where she had stood and pointed them out, her nails were scarlet-painted talons gleaming wetly in the surrounding gray. Every night she had hovered over them, the tiny brush glossing on stature and sensuality with red varnish. Filed them, creamed them, trimmed them, long red nails as if they were weapons instead of fragile and useless decoration. Leaving scratches on his back, marks that faded and dissolved quickly, only temporary remnants of her.

The pigs did not whoof or exchange exclamations and questions; they did not address her at all but snorted and munched steadily to each other.

Finished her work, she closed the door gently instead of slamming it, her fingers lingering on the cold iron handle. They waited until they heard her footsteps before they broke into a chorus of whoofings, shaking their heads and rubbing themselves against the fences. The one in the second pen put her forelegs on the top of her fence and scrambled upright, leading into a long chorus of excited whoofs and snorts while the others cocked their heads to listen.

Going up the hill to the house, she heard a faint echo of their discussion and suddenly wanted to turn and go back, speak to them in the strawy dimness. She stopped abruptly, listened to the surrounding silence of impending winter, then continued up the hill to the house.

He would always stop and listen outside the door, her father, blue eyes scanning the sky endlessly. Looking up to the sky or down at the ground, never straight ahead. Soon she would be like that, she thought, watching her booted feet climb the hill.

In the cramped, blue-painted bathroom off the kitchen, she stared intently at herself in the narrow mirror. Hair rumpled and coarse, face bony and angular. Screwing up her eyes, she rubbed her hand hard over her nose and forehead. "Come on," she said to her reflection in the mirror. "You've got to do something. You just can't let things go. You haven't been off the yard for weeks." Her image faced her, stolid and unwinking. "Talking to yourself yet," she said.

She stared a long time trying to remember her other face, Judith with hair falling to her shoulders, eyes outlined and shaded, lips colored. Expression as calm as glass, smiling at everyone in turn, at him so much like the others, her eyes did not even crinkle for him, lips unmoving, not a hint of their bruised swollenness or the dark crescent on her upper arm, the bright mark on her neck.

Now her face was pale and colorless, hair short and ragged. More familiar than any image of herself, her mother's motion of passing her hand over her face, erasing something there. And it was her mother's face, smooth and younger, looking back at her from the mirror.

"Can I go outside now?" Her mother turned from the mirror on the wall, fingers pursing her lips, hand moving from brow to chin, wearily molding it back, back into place. She touched her hair nervously then sighed. "Sweep the floor first, Judy."

And after she swept the floor she ran outside and held her face into the wind, knowing it would never be like her mother's, she would never try to smooth it clear like that, so desperate and exposed.

Judith started. "Hell," she said, turning quickly away from the mirror. She thrust the plug into the tub and ran a steaming bath instead of the cursory showers she took every day. Refusing to move, she swished the water between her legs until it was no longer hot. Judith lying in the tub after the door closed behind him, sloughing her chafed skin in hot soapy water, passing her hands over her body to reassure it, still whole. She scrubbed her hair until she felt it squeak under her hands, rubbed herself with a towel until her skin ached, then dressed quickly, purposefully.

The steering wheel of the car felt strange and cold under her hands; it seemed almost to be maneuvering her. So different, driving on graveled country roads, no lines, no hemming cars. It had frightened Judith to drive in the city during rush hour. She always took the bus, liking the wait at the shelter, its ritual of stop and start. Sitting on the lengthwise seats, reading and rereading the ads as the bus lumbered through the press of frantic cars. The comforting bus; everyone unobtrusive with the unwritten rules of morning commuters. Ten minutes to collect herself in its humming calm before the long day, the desk, the typewriter. Even so, she saw him everywhere, in shaving-cream ads, in the dark-haired man three seats down, in someone waiting at a corner for the light to change, briefcase in hand and trenchcoat buttoned and precise. So common, she could not rid herself of his recurring image.

The low sports car was difficult to control on the ridged, bumpy gravel. She sighed as she swung onto the highway. Riding between them, mother and father on either side of her, the road straight ahead for miles, trees whipping by. Judy leaned back against the seat and stretched her feet in front of her, newly shined shoes pointing up. She could touch them both—her father's iron leg shifting on the gas pedal, her mother's soft thigh through the cotton skirt. Matrixed there, she fixed her eyes on the disappearing road, everything so perfectly balanced it was unbearable, she was the center of the world.

In town, Judith drove around for half an hour. It was familiar, the same as every farming center: one long street lined with stores, side streets with garages and machinery shops before they edged into blocks of houses stretching to the hospital and the golf course. *Ben Hur* was playing at the only movie theater. *Ben Hur*. She remembered her mother ironing; Norman sat sideways on a kitchen chair talking to her while he waited. She slipped by him, barely saying hello in her hurry to get upstairs. He always came too early. She was angry when he caught her in chore clothes, coming in from cleaning the pigs. She knew the satisfied half-smile he turned after her retreating back, thinking she was his, poised on his chair to swallow her, his body in an attitude of possession.

"Make sure you're not too late," from her mother.

On the road just out of sight of the house he stopped the car. "How about a kiss?" She bent toward him dutifully, feeling like a wife, then wiped her mouth with the back of her hand. In the movie she could feel his fingers leaving marks on the sleeve of her white blouse, her own fingers prying his hand off her leg while he whispered to her, "Judy, Judy . . ."

She drove from dealer to dealer. There were six of them in town. Finally she pulled into the used-car lot behind Macleods filled with Ford pickups. She had learned to drive in the Ford half-ton, her father close beside her shouting instructions as they bounced over the summer fallow. Its surliness was part of its dependability; it always started no matter how cold it was.

She parked the car and walked around the lot, looking at the trucks, prices scrawled on the windshields. She wished she knew more, it was confusing; they were all the same to her, some lower and longer, others heavy or high. She settled on a stubby blue half-ton that had an air of having been well used but carefully used. Asked all the requisite questions: mileage, former owner, horsepower; even though she she was helpless to verify the salesman's answers. Took it for a test drive twice around the block, listening to the engine. The truck seemed steady and reliable. Her instincts told her to take it.

When she jumped to the ground and slammed the truck door, the salesman came out of the mobile office, his round face smiling. She interrupted his affable, "Well, how did you like . . ." by pointing at the MG.

"Straight trade."

"Oh well, young lady, I don't think I can do that. This truck is worth at least a thousand more."

She shook her head. "No deal. That MG is a $5,000 car. Straight trade or nothin'."

"Well," he scratched his head, disturbing the few strands of hair carefully plastered across the top. "I'd better ask the boss." He turned back to the office.

"I haven't got all day," she said.

He waved his hand at her, disappeared through the door. She leaned against the MG, hands flat on either side of her on the red surface.

Judith standing close beside him, his eyes lingering over the low car. Like his eyes on her naked back, the same insatiable hunger, so masculine, that instant desire, she wanted to clutch his arm, insist that she was different from the lines of the car.

"Like it?" He turned to her with a slow smile.

Shrugging, she was careful to hide the contempt she felt for his covetousness. "It's nice."

She walked away a few steps and stood waiting for him, furious, daring herself to keep walking down the street, to leave him with the car, leave him with everything.

She felt rather than heard him come up behind her and take her arm. Laughing, he turned her around, walked her back to the MG, the driver's side, opened the door for her, handed her the keys. He settled down in the low seat beside her. "Let's go for a ride."

"This is stupid," she said. "You're not going to buy it anyway."

"There you are wrong, my little one." He touched her nose with his finger, mocking. "I've already decided to."

"You're crazy."

He laughed again, the smoothness of his face dissolving into the lines he would wear permanently in a few years, creases around his eyes. "No. Happy Birthday."

She looked at him, again that well of fury inside her. "You're not giving me this car," she said flatly.

"Oh? Well, I already have."

"I won't take it." Her knuckles strained white on the steering wheel.

"Well, my dear." He leaned toward her,

turned her face to his and touched her lips. "You're wrong because, you see, you have no choice. I have never bought you flowers, chocolates or perfume, so you must accept this to make up for it."

Staring at him, the depths of his steely gray eyes, she suddenly knew he was right and something turned over inside her. So smoothly, so effortlessly, he had amalgamated them, her and the car, the car and the woman.

The salesman struggled across the lot again, his breath white against the air. "Well, dear," he said, "you're in luck today. The boss is in a good mood. We'll trade you the truck for the MG and five hundred dollars."

She looked at him evenly. "No deal. Straight trade."

"But we can't . . ."

"Okay." She turned to the car. "I'll go somewhere else."

"Wait." He rubbed his hands together. "Really, don't you see . . ."

"No," she said, tightly humorless, "I don't." She opened the car, slid her legs in and slammed the door. Backing out, she cursed the salesman for a wasted hour, then had to slam on her brakes as he almost flung himself in front of her.

Beaming, he was puffing from running across the lot. "It's a deal. It's a deal!"

She climbed out of the car. "Almost too late," she said. "Better not hold out so long next time."

"But I have to take it for a test drive."

"Go ahead, I've got all day."

Funny how she had slipped so easily into that callous urban pragmatism, swiftly manipulative. She had thought that she would shed that first, but it was still there, somewhere inside her.

She threw the accumulation of the MG's glove compartment into a garbage can—ticket stubs, programs, one of his gloves. Almost stopped to retrieve it, that glove, then backed away. Nothing, she wanted nothing left. She walked away from the MG gleaming red in front of the dealer's office to the stolid and patient blue truck, clenching her hands against the ache to go back to that Judith, hair flying in the wind on a Saturday drive, the rough blanket under her back in the park, his hands down the sides of her body. She flung herself into the truck and slammed the door, started it to the reassurance of a low rumble. She was free, no more the car and the woman. Why couldn't she laugh? And then she had trouble with the gear shift, knew she should have settled for an automatic instead of a standard.

At IGA she bought a month's groceries. In Norberg she could get bread and milk but anything else was outrageous. The IGA was filled with afternoon town housewives, hair perfectly carved into place, their fur coats dangling over the shopping carts. She shopped hurriedly, feeling alien and ashamed of her casual slacks and ski jacket, still conscious of the careful dress she had so recently deserted.

At the Rexall drugstore she stopped for liquid iron for the baby piglets. Her father had always bought it at the vet clinic on the outskirts of town, stopping there on the way home. She would scramble out of the truck after him into the cries of dogs and pigs and horses and cows impounded in a strange place. The vet came out of the back room, white coat bloody, to nod at her father. "Hello, Jim, how's the pigs?" Her father grunted, a man's reply.

"Buggers keep me busy. Need some aureomycin, feraustin, oh, and a couple of bottles of erysipelas vaccine."

Behind the front desk, the vet's wife reached into her drawer. "Would you like a candy, Judy?"

Judy looked up at her father. He nodded at her and she reached for the box the gray-haired woman held out. "Thank you," she whispered, rubbing her hand against the side of her green skirt for town; she hated green, such an ugly color.

The vet's wife got up and beckoned. "Come here, we've got something special in the back."

Judy followed her carefully, slowly—Would she see blood?—down some steps into a large bright room with a steel table. In the corner the vet's wife turned and there was a white, curly-haired goat, small and nervous, on dainty feet. Judy came closer and the goat put his head down and butted at her.

The vet's wife laughed. "He wants to play."

"Is he sick?" Judy asked.

"No, he's all better now." She smiled and her teeth gleamed white under red lipstick.

Judy was sure the goat would die. Waiting for her father, she wondered if they had cut him open already.

The green-painted clinic was gone now; a gas station had taken its place. And it was no longer on the outskirts; the town stretched far beyond it. In Woolworths she looked at sweaters and blue jeans but finally bought herself a checkered flannel shirt to wear as a nightshirt. Sleeping with the window open to the cold air, her thin nightgowns seemed ridiculous.

It felt strange to be walking among people again, feeling her face as blind and anonymous as theirs. And strange to be shopping when there was nothing that she needed now. Once shopping had been a constant activity, something to keep up with. She brushed between the people without noticing them;

through her own isolation they had passed into insignificance. And there, in the middle of that farmer's town, she felt a sudden surge of self-reliance, a small spurt of self-respect that gave her an instant and brilliant hope. So that she could afford to ignore them, the people around her; she had herself and that was enough.

Finally ready to go home, she had to struggle to get the truck into reverse, putting both hands on the stick and straining with all her might. "Damn, damn, damn," she said, heedless of the faces that turned toward her from the sidewalk. At last it slipped into gear and she could back out of her parking space. She should have tried reverse on the test drive but hadn't; damn, another awkward mistake.

Driving out of town she watched, as if from a great distance, the people on the crosswalks, bodies bent against the wind. It felt strange to be in the truck, so high compared to the MG; she was looking down at people instead of up at them. She had to stretch her legs to reach the pedals just enough to tire her muscles, but taking the short cut home on the gravel instead of the highway, she was satisfied that the truck held well to the road. It felt as solid and dependable under her hands as the car had seemed vulnerable to flying rocks and the ditches.

At the Norberg road she hesitated, then braked and turned. She hadn't been there since she moved to the farm. Maybe there would be mail, a letter from the lawyer, or from him. . . .

In the five o'clock gloom three boys were flooding the uncovered skating rink beside the curved steel roof of the pre-fab curling rink. Faded letters over the door proclaimed a large, paint-peeling building as the Scandinavian National Hall. The village was little more than a long gray street of old and abandoned false-fronted stores and a large, two-story hotel. Like her old hometown, the empty buildings outnumbered the occupied ones: a low, ghostly creamery, dark, boarded-up garage, sagging bank, and railway station abandoned—only a freight once a week. Even the occupied buildings were divided. The school edged away at the north end of town and the Lutheran church at the south, a denomination to itself. In the middle of main street the hotel presided, pickups and cars angle-parked in front of it. The bottom half of the tavern windows were curtained to prevent town children from peeking in. The door of the tavern was open and Judith could almost hear the hum of activity within.

Even beside the hotel, the post office kept itself separate. It wore a somewhat forlorn air of expectancy. NORBERG the red-and-white government sign read. POST OFFICE.

Judy would bounce up and down on the front seat while her mother went in to check the box, coming out again with a handful of papers and letters that Judy could slit open with a table knife for her father that night, carefully, one by one, waiting until he had read each before opening another.

She left the truck on and ran around the front of it. The door of the post office sprang shut behind her and she was in a tiny, square lobby with a community bulletin board, a large, geranium-filled window across from a wall of numbered mailboxes, and one wicket in a wooden partition. So similar to that other post office, Judy standing on tiptoe to reach their box and turn the key; her mother talking to Mr. Belling while she took the letters out, one by one.

The spectacled man sitting at the desk behind the counter rose when she peered through the wicket. "Is there any mail under General Delivery for Judith Pierce, please?"

Fingers hooked in his suspenders, he shuffled to the row of wooden boxes against the far wall and thumbed through a stack of envelopes under "P." Extracting two from the pile, he crept across the floor again to lay them on the counter. Liver spots danced patterns over the backs of his hands.

"Oh," she said. "I didn't really expect anything."

He raised thick white brows at her, eyes weak and watery behind the round spectacles, but said nothing.

"Well, thank you."

He nodded and scuffed back to his desk, pulled out his chair and sat down heavily.

She let the door slip from her hand and slam. "Didn't say a goddamn word," she muttered as she thrust the truck into second. Well, some kind of mail. Somebody knew she was there.

In the kitchen she tore the ends open then shrugged. No letters. What could you expect? A circular from a feed company asking to buy their pre-mixed feed. And a form from Statistics Canada, Agriculture Division. Picking up a pencil, she sat down and idly read the questions: Type of farming. Size of farm. Number of head of livestock. Acres under cultivation. Location. She wrote carefuly to answer in full—Central Alberta Hog Farmer.

"My father is a pig farmer." Judith said it aloud, surprised at her own temerity, her desire to shock them out of their prissy complacency.

They looked at her in dead silence, finicky and wellkept hands curled around ceramic coffee mugs. Like pretty grubs, white and dead, she thought, facing them with a half-smile on her face.

Sherry took a dainty swallow. "Did you grow up on the farm?"

"Of course." Judith egged her to say more, to ask, to ask.

"Did you slop pigs and everything?" asked round-eyed Mary Lou.

Eyeing her coolly, Judith nodded, waited.

"Well, aren't they dirty, crawling in the mud all the time, don't they smell?" She wrinkled her nose and shuddered.

Judith allowed herself a long breathless laugh at their vapid talk. "Of course not, dummy," she said cruelly. "Farming is a totally mechanized operation now. They're all kept in pens, perfectly clean, and they don't smell at all. They're cleaner than you or me."

"But . . ." Their faces turned upwards to her as she stood.

"Back to work," she said lightly, swishing her cool, silky body away, savoring their looks, their imminent expressions—"A pig farm!" "Can you believe it?"—and she laughed as she rested her long fingers on the typewriter keys.

It looked strange on the Statistics Canada form, as if it were really another person who was the pig farmer. Her father had always refused to answer them, tearing the brown envelopes across with stubby fingers before he opened them, refusing even to read the questions. "Goddamn government, always trying to find out what you're doing so they can tell you what to do next."

"And how the hell did the government find out I'm farming?" she asked the Canadian Imperial Bank of Commerce scenery on the wall. "Snoopy bastards." But she put the form in the return envelope and propped it on the desk. Maybe she would mail it next time she went to Norberg. See if the postmaster talked at all. Grouchy old codger.

It was dark already. Dusk falling earlier and earlier, the days were shortening themselves by inches. She pushed her chair back from the desk and stretched, then shivered and went to change into jeans and a thick sweater. She had been gone almost all day; the barn and the pigs seemed remote and distant. Pulling on her boots, she did not hear the truck drive into the yard and the sudden knock at the door jolted her. She went to answer it apprehensively, wondering if she would have to keep a dog to warn her of intruders.

He grinned casually when she opened the door, head tipped back and his hands in his pockets. "Oh, it's you," she said. What was his name—Ed? Ed Something?

"Yeah," he said. "Didn't expect me so soon again, didja?"

"No."

"Bought a half-ton, eh? Good idea."

"Well, I thought so," she said dryly. "Kinda hard to carry pigs in an MG."

He guffawed appreciatively. "Thought you'd get rid of that toy. Well, I just came over to say the missus told me to come and ask you to supper Saturday."

Surprised, she hesitated. The flap of the upper pocket on his checkered jacket was tucked into the pocket itself. "I'm sorry," she said. "I've forgotten your name."

"Ed Stamby. Got the place two miles down the road."

"Oh yes. Well, that's really nice of her but I don't want to be a bother."

"No bother," he said, turning to go. "She wouldn't ask if she didn't want to have you. Six-thirty tomorrow then."

She was annoyed that he took her hedging for acceptance but could not think of a graceful way to call him back and refuse. Shrugging her shoulders, she pulled on her coat and trudged down the hill to the barn while he drove away leaving his exhaust to hang in the chilly air.

The cold crept into her, exhilarating, made her want to run. She remembered running through the late winter light to the barn, to him. Her feet followed the path like a dancer's score, every bump and hollow, she never stumbled. Inside the door, she would wait a moment to let the steamy air settle on her, penetrate her skin.

"Daddy?"

"Is that you, Judy?" he called from the back of the barn.

"Yes, I'm home." She picked up her shovel and pitchfork and carried them to the first pen, the ritual as comforting as an old shirt.

"How was school?"

"Okay." She rested her small hand on the sow's rough back, pushing into the solid flesh; the pig moved beneath it, turgid as earth.

After the day in town, Judith entered the barn's loomy redolence eagerly. She was whole here, a part of their tumescent sanctuary of female warmth. It was that, their femaleness, the subtle scent that lifted from beneath their alert tails, surrounding her like a soothing conspiracy. Expectant, they pressed forward against their fences, eyes glowing under the naked light bulbs. Transformed and spellbinding they surrounded her like priestesses of her creed. They had been waiting for her.

Four

Surprised at her own anticipation, Judith did chores early the next night. The sows were puzzled; they edged about their pens rejecting the impermanence of a different time, their schedule destroyed. She worked carefully but too quickly. In her hurry they sensed an eagerness for something they did not have and could not give to her. Instinctively they knew that she would go to other humans tonight, and they felt vaguely disappointed. The best part of her was her aloneness; she did not carry the acrid smell of humans who mingled with each other constantly. But there was a subtle excitement in her quick movements that transmitted itself to them and pleased them.

While she forked straw and scraped the pens clean with the shovel, they ate, quietly and watchfully. Tossing the last forkful on top of the pile, she trundled the wheelbarrow full of rank straw out the door with a kind of flourish they might even have smiled at.

"Okay," she said, back inside, closing the door behind her.

At the sound of her voice they stood perfectly still, waiting. Almost embarrassed, she said nothing more, but walked up and down the aisle a few minutes looking at them, hands in her coat pockets. Their heads followed her movement with relentless curiosity; she had always done her work and nothing more. In her movement there was a compressed nervousness that silenced them; utterly still, they absorbed her smell and the sound of her rubber boots squeaking on the cement floor, noted the angle of her head and her ragged hair.

When she was gone, they pawed the straw into thick nests of warmth, snorting at each other. But there was a quietness in them and they sprawled at rest finally with a hazy trust in each other's breathing and in the clean straw they lay upon. Her straw. They knew that now, knew it with certainty and relish.

"Give them lots of straw, Judy," her father would say, "They like it."

In the house she hung up her coat, then stripped and showered quickly. Facing herself in the mirror she rejected makeup; no reason for it anyway—Ed Stamby and wife. And hadn't he said something about sons—probably a couple of gawking teenage boys.

Dressing, she could not conquer a feeling of strangeness, the texture of the blue wool dress alien. Once on, it bound her movements, made her awkward and constrained, heavy. She smoothed the dress over the outline of her thighs, then turned from the mirror abruptly. "Well," she told herself, "you can't wear blue jeans."

Driving the truck was worse, the very pedals resisted the pressure of her heeled slippers; and by the time she maneuvered into the Stamby's yard her knees felt weak. Tilted forward, Judith's body moved to that slightly off-balance rhythm, edging her around an interior world. On the sidewalks she hurried to be inside, balanced again, heels on corridor and carpet. That deliberate forward thrust for the push of her breasts and the curve of her calves, she knew it and carefully practiced her tottering gait.

Even before she was out of the truck they opened the door, light from the doorway streaming into what she could see was a well-kept yard. Ed stood there, saying, "Come on in, come on in," and she had no time to hesitate. Steering her into the living room, he said boisterously, "Boys, here she is—our genuine farmerette from down the road, Judith Pierce."

"Hello," she said coolly.

They were not gangling teenagers but three handsome, big-boned men rising to the full height of their long legs and broad shoulders, looking down at her with windburnt faces, brown eyes under curly brown hair that stuck up despite punishment with water.

"These are my three sons, John and Jim and Jerry." It sounded like a joke and she looked at Ed quickly; there was nothing in his face but sincerity. She extended her hand to each of them in turn, wondering which was which. Looked at them, so ordinarily attractive, so fresh somehow, the tinge of innocent arrogance they carried, like Norman so sure of his rightness, his just cause and his claim. Fighting him, she had always fought the weight of him, pushing her into places she refused to be in, laughing. "Judy, you're a tease," when she had to quell a desperate desire to beat at his square face with her hands.

Studying them covertly, she almost expected round straw hats and a blue tinge to appear, like some painting of strong young men. So that the brownness of the short, fine-boned woman suddenly standing in front of them made her blink, an incongruity in the picture, a patch of contrast in that maze of men, years and years of men swarming and shouldering through her outline.

Judith struggled to place the woman and wondered if, in that confusion, she had already been introduced and then forgotten. Behind a fringe of brownish-gray hair and large, round-framed glasses, her eyes smiled quietly.

"I'm Mina," she said, holding out a hand as small as Judith's own but tanned and hard. "And I know you're Judith."

"Yes, I am," she said. "Hello." Ed's daughter or his wife? she wondered while Mina took her coat from her and carried it to a bedroom. Impossible to say. She moved as if she were the only woman in the house yet free from it. Incredible to think of her as being the mother of those three young men, their very finger bones coarser than her wrists and arms.

Ed was seated in a big green reclining chair, watching Hockey Night in Canada on the color television at the end of the room. The sons sprawled on the chesterfield, at ease but eyeing her covertly, this woman. Just so had she felt Norman's eyes always on her, every movement clocked, Judy reaching to tie her shoe, to pull on her coat, each slip of skin and muscle passing under his eyes.

"Sit down and make yourself at home," Ed said.

"Thanks, but I'll see if I can help with anything." She followed Mina into the huge bright kitchen where the table stood set for six. So she was the only woman in the house. She tried with difficulty to picture it. How old was she. Thirty? Forty? Fifty? She stared at her, the brownish woman in dark-blue slacks and flowered blue blouse, standing at the huge white stove stirring gravy.

Mina turned and smiled at her suddenly, catching her off guard. Judith was hesitant, had expected this woman to be like all women, like the secretaries, the typists, her schoolmates, a common denominator. She had come prepared to give polite and acceptable answers to all the inevitable female questions, curious and probing but fundamentally disinterested in her replies, waiting to make their own answers.

"You're making out all right," said Mina. The statement was more than just that; it showed an unexpectedly comforting awareness of her aloneness two miles down the road. Judith could not decide whether to like this or not, but she surprised herself by her own truthfulness.

"Yes, but it's kind of lonely right now." Damn, she thought, don't say that or you'll have this woman over every day. Not to mention those guys.

Over the squadron of saucepans on the stove, Mina looked at her seriously. "Maybe," she said, "but it must be nice not to have people charging in on you all the time."

"Yeah, you must be pretty busy."

Mina nodded. "Between the chickens and the men." She jerked her head at the living room. "It's great when they're all out on the back quarter of the third section."

She could not hold back a giggle. "You're certainly outnumbered."

Mina lowered her voice. "I kept trying to have girls, or there wouldn't be three of them. After the third one I quit. I couldn't risk having five men around." She shrugged and spread her hands, then stirred again.

Her mother had stood just so, legs apart, hands hovering over steaming and bubbling pots and pans, a delicate orchestration of vegetables and sauces.

"Don't forget the salt, Judy." Moving in circumference around her mother's world: the stove, the sewing machine, the washer. Every request simple and familiar, repeated at paced intervals, an unvarying rhythm. Reliable. But her father's demands were complex, frightening in their dimension. And she knew there was more to it than just a simple accomplishing of her task; he expected so much more, her father.

So Mina was Ed's wife and the mother of those men. She almost wanted to laugh at her, she was so comic, so quietly and unassumingly direct. "So you quit trying?"

"Yes. But I miss seeing another woman—I grew up in a family of nine girls. And most of the women around here . . . Well, I guess I'm the weird bird, not them. It would be nice to have someone interesting down the road though."

And even as she was pleased and said eagerly, "Yes, it will," she was holding back.

Judith always alone, no telephone conversations or shopping trips or lunches with them. Carrying herself aloof and intact even as she moved among them, coffee and shop-talk but no revelations. Secretly she despised them, pear-shaped women who grew from chairs behind desks, even as she knew herself to be one of them, was becoming pear-shaped, beginning to associate herself with her desk, her typewriter.

"You've been to Norberg, I guess," Mina said.

"Yes." Judith sat down on one of the kitchen chairs. She could not stop staring at Mina.

"What did you think?"

"Just like the town where I grew up."

"All these small towns are the same, aren't they?"

"Is there much to do here?"

Mina shrugged, mashing potatoes. "Curling, skating, a dance once in a while, a school play. The bar. You have to make your own excitement." She brought the dished-up dinner to the table in a series of quick, bird-like swoops that the men seemed to recognize; they appeared and ranged themselves around the table.

The slightest of them, maybe the youngest, cleared his throat and somewhat awkwardly held a chair for her.

"Draggin' out your company manners, eh, Jim?" Ed Stamby boomed. She looked at Jim quickly, his dark, laughing face, dimples, mobile lips. He sat down across from her and surreptitiously winked at her, the corners of his mouth twitching with an unformed smile. She felt suddenly a connection, an unspoken tension with him, almost as if he had touched her in some secret place.

"He *should* hold her chair," Mina said to Ed. "You wouldn't."

"Oh, Mina, if Judy here can handle sows, I'm sure she can pull out her own chair."

She sensed a hidden conflict by Mina's set lips, and she said quickly, "Most people call me Judith."

"Judith." He had formed her name softly, lips and tongue caressing it. Looking at her he said it again, so that she felt her face warm, blushing. "You have a good name."

"Thank you." She looked down at her hands.

"Well, would you like some wine?"

"At lunch?"

"Why not?" He smiled. "Nothing is too good for my new assistant."

She liked that, being called an assistant instead of a secretary.

He cleared his throat. "I asked you to lunch because it's impossible to talk to you at the office. I wanted to apologize for the other evening."

She lifted her eyes from the elaborately folded fan of the cloth napkin. Under the table she felt his leg brush against hers, the feel of his rough trousers through her stocking. "It's not necessary."

"Well . . ." He spread his hands, square, blunt, well-manicured. They had strength, Judith thought, but a strength rather more cruel than gentle. "I just wanted to touch you all of a sudden. I must be crazy, but you just looked so—what can I say?—vulnerable. No, that's not it either," he amended quickly. "More . . . receptive, I guess."

"It doesn't matter," she said, knowing that she should protest. Still, she could not; under his careful scrutiny, his impeccable advance, she almost apologized to him.

Ed refused to give in. "Why do they call you Judith?"

"Because I don't like being called Judy."

"Why?" He was insistent.

"Because I'm not a kid."

"So we really can't call you Judy?" Jim asked teasingly.

Sobbing against his shoulder, her small, pajama-clad body huddled into her father's warm bulk. "Judy, Judy, shhh," he said. "Don't cry now, I'm here . . ." The candle stuck in the saucer was a tiny star in the dark kitchen. There was another flash and another clap of thunder. She jumped at the sound, clutching him, and the candle flame flickered. He put a big rough hand over her ear. "It's only noise, Judy, it's only noise. I'll take care of you. Listen to the rain singing."

"No," she said pleasantly to Jim, "you cannot call me Judy."

They all glanced at her quickly, too quickly, and then away, back down to their plates. Jim cut his chicken carefully, and she knew an instant of repentance for hurting his feelings.

"Do you curl?" She turned toward the voice that asked, grateful for his rescue.

"No, but I guess I could learn how. Is it hard?"

"It's easy. I'll teach you." He seemed somehow the oldest, stooped a little as if he carried an invisible burden.

"Here, here, I'm better at it than you are, John," said Jim jealously.

The tension broken, Judith laughed at him. "I can't promise to go curling. My pigs come first."

"How many do you have?" John asked.

"Only ten, yet."

"Just sows?"

"Yes."

Mina was passing bowls and platters and ladling sauce but she said nothing, only smiled at Judith now and then as if in encouragement.

"Are they all due soon?" Jerry asked.

"Pretty soon. The breeder said they were due from the middle of November until about the end of December. Anytime now.

"Can you manage?" Jim interrupted.

"I think so," she said dryly, wanting to make a face at him. "I only helped my father until I was eighteen."

"Well, if you need any help, just call on me!" He winked at her again and she had to smile at him even as she saw the dangerous light under his disarming dimples, knew that he could upset her balance.

But she wanted to stop talking about her pigs; she had an irrational fear that every spoken word was dangerous to her enterprise. She turned to Mina. "Does the school offer any adult courses at night?"

Mina pushed up her glasses. "Sometimes," she said softly.

"It's usually cake decorating and sewing or ceramics," Ed said.

"Have you ever taken any of them?" she asked Mina.

"No."

"If you want to," Ed said, "I could get you the forms."

"Well . . ." Judith wrinkled her nose. "Not cake decorating or ceramics, and I can sew pretty good already."

She remembered her mother stooped behind the machine, moving the orange cloth expertly. Under her fingers Judy's dresses grew magically.

"Do *you* sew?" she asked Mina.

Ed pulled at his sleeve. "She made this shirt."

Mina smiled at Judith and stood up. "Does everyone want ice cream on their apple pie?"

After coffee Ed scraped back his chair.

"Come and watch the end of the hockey game with us," Jim said. "Jerry'll dry the dishes."

"I don't have to watch it." She smiled. "The Canadiens will win." She took the striped dish towel out of Jerry's hand. "Come on, I want to help."

Jim leaned in the living room doorway, amused and inquisitive, watching them both. Quickly Jerry turned away and went out the back door, pulling on a jacket. Jim laughed. "Hey, he's developed an instant crush on you." She looked at him blankly, then turned to the sink, her back toward him. Even so, she could still feel his laughing eyes intent on her face.

"Jerry's so quiet and glum compared to the other two," Mina said, running hot water. "I guess that's because he's the youngest, never could get a word in edgewise."

"How old is he?" she asked idly, drying a glass.

"Twenty-one. When I look at Jim, he's four years older, but what a difference. He just takes over everything. Always running around, loves to talk, chasing after girls, even high school kids. I keep thinking sometime he'll knock up some sweet little sixteen-year-old and that'll be it."

She glanced at Mina, surprised.

Mina laughed. "Don't look so shocked. That's what he's like. Who knows better than me that he comes in at four in the morning and leaves used condoms under the car seat?"

Judith fumbled for an answer. "What about John then?" This woman had a funny attitude toward her sons.

"Oh, he's steady and collected. A plodder. Been going out with the same girl for five years and still hasn't asked her to marry him. I expect he will soon, unless he finds somebody he likes better."

Was she matchmaking? Judith wondered. And two sons, a choice yet! No wonder the dinner invitation had come so quickly. Shit. And she'd even liked this woman.

Mina smiled at her as if she read her thoughts. "I expect they'll bug you," she said, "but don't let them talk you into anything. Just tell them to go to hell."

Startled, Judith threw back her head and laughed as she had not laughed for weeks. Mina joined her.

"Hey, what's the joke?" Jim called from the living room.

"We're talking about you," Mina answered.

He poked his head into the kitchen. "What a nice topic of conversation. Are you almost done? It's getting pretty fast."

"We're coming."

In the living room they watched the end of the hockey game without much conversation. Mina curled up in a corner chair that had a stack of library books beside it, listening with her hands folded. John and Jim teased Judith, who answered instinctively, alert to the familiar game, her replies swift and easy.

Glancing toward the corner chair she glimpsed a brown framed picture of Mina pushing her glasses up on her nose. Funny that she wouldn't talk around the men, only alone. And what was it about her that was so attractive? Nothing noticeable.

With the excuse that she had to get up in the morning, Judith stood to take her leave early. They all came to the door, engulfing her hand in turn while Mina fetched her coat. "Thank you," she said to Mina, looking directly into those still, brown eyes. And surprised at her own sincerity, added, "I really enjoyed it."

"Goodbye." They were grinning at her, that row of men, and she could feel Jim's eyes resting on her face.

"See you," said Mina. And turning at the door, Judith saw her startling gamin smile appear as she stood there, not even reaching the shoulders of the two men on either side of her.

She ground her gears and was embarrassed, swore as she drove out of their yard. Their faces wavered in a hazy arrangement before her eyes as, in the rearview mirror, the yard light faded behind her.

Five

The bare branches of the poplar trees to the east of the house creaked and groaned under the impact of a harsh north wind. In the dream she and Mina drove the half-ton down a country road green with the summer leaves of trees. The pigs were in the back of the truck; she could hear them squealing and snorting as they drove along. Then suddenly he was driving, too fast, the MG swaying from side to side on the gravel road. "Wait," she shouted, clutching his arm. "Wait. The pigs . . ."

The pigs. She sat up in bed, covers falling away from her, and the warmth trapped under the flannel shirt receding from her skin. She hadn't checked them last night when she got home from the Stambys. She shivered and rubbed her arms; the chill in the air was different somehow. And then she saw, beyond the square window of her bedroom, an inch of snow lying on the ground.

The pigs. Was the barn warm enough, was the furnace working? She jumped out of bed, slammed the window shut. Pulling on only a shirt and blue jeans, she plunged through the house, gray with the dimness of a snow morning: her oblong, unused living room, the scattered kitchen. In the porch she flung on coat and boots so quickly as to hardly notice before she was out the door and in the cold air.

Prickly and chilling, the wind lifted the

hair of her neck. She stopped, looked at the sky the way her father had always done. And could feel the air different, holding a soft wetness that shone in the morning half-light. The curve of the horizon hummed with it, everywhere the luminescence of the snow. It had run itself over everything like a soothing touch, rounding and softening the most angular objects. She stood quietly, feeling it soften her too. Then, no longer hurrying, she scuffed her way through it to the barn, kicking stiff-legged, feeling the hard uneven ground on the soles of her feet.

Awakening while the house was still quiet, daylight not yet arrived, Judy crept downstairs in her stocking feet, feeling her way along the railing in the semidarkness. Through the kitchen window it glowed with a pale phosphorescence, a radiant invitation. She tied her running shoes, zipped up her hooded red parka and slipped out, closing the door behind her softly, so softly. Anticipating the clean expanse of yard she stood breathing lightly, quickly, already the sting of windless cold on her cheeks. Then with a sudden, soundless cry she flung herself into it, heedless, flat on her back, arms flailing and legs scissoring. Carefully she got up and, standing on one leg, jumped away from the imprint there to an unmarked spot. Again she flung herself down, again flailed and scissored the shape, already feeling the dampness creeping through the seat of her pants to her skin. Again and again, jumping from one angel to create another, she pressed them into the mold of the snow with her body. Until they were everywhere, hardly a square yard of untouched snow left. Angels, robed and winged, lifting themselves magically in the smooth bluish layer. Wet and shivering then, she ran to the door, looked back once to make sure she had done it, that it wasn't a dream. And crept inside, so quiet, so cold, her wet feet tracking, to fall asleep on the kitchen floor until she felt her father's arms around her lifting her up against the heat of his body, carrying her back to bed.

"Did you see?" she mumbled into his shoulder.

"Yes." He pulled the blankets up to her chin. "I saw a million angels."

On her way to the barn the snow gathered and capped the toes of her black boots like a decoration. She laughed suddenly and the laugh was smoothed and curved by the snow. Leaning over, she printed her open and gloveless hand on the unmarked white. Between the heat of her fingers it was rough and grainy, so cold her hand ached instantly. She rubbed her hand against her blue-jeaned legs, then against her crotch, feeling the cool wetness slip through the denim into her skin and leaving a flush of heat beneath it.

Standing at the office window she watched the flakes falling past her, falling without her and beyond her. When she turned he was leaning in his open doorway, watching. "Sorry," she said, sliding onto her typing stool, bending her head against his gaze.

"Put on your coat." He walked to the rack, lifted her coat. "Here." He held it for her, gave her no choice. She stood awkwardly, arms hanging. "Put on your boots," he said. She had to sit down to tug them on, polished leather over her stockinged legs. He leaned on her desk and pressed her buzzer. "Clara, Judith and I are going out to see about the Hyte contract. Can you please take the calls." He came out of his office shrugging into his overcoat, dark blue tweed, then turned back and came out again with his briefcase. "Ready?"

She followed him, almost stumbling, knotting the belt of her coat. Alone in the elevator he smiled at her. "Well, aren't you going to say anything?" She shook her head, could not look at him. Outside, the snow struck soft blows against her face and ungloved hands, clung to her hair.

She walked beside him to his car—the same slate gray as his eyes—touched the surface with her hand, smoothed a patch clear. He held the door open and she slid inside, out of the soft envelope of snow.

Driving, encased together, they said nothing. Judith leaned back, staring into the vortex of whirling flakes that flung themselves against the windshield, allowing herself to be hypnotized. In the park, he turned the ignition off, went around to open her door. His voice was rough. "Come on, let's walk."

Into the driving snow they staggered together but separate, not touching or speaking. He carried a tight, narrowed look, almost wincing. Judith held her face into the snow-driven wind until it was numb, beyond numbness, tears freezing on her cheeks. An hour they wandered aimlessly in the mid-week deserted park, the only movement in a landscape where the snow was sculpting everything into its winter posture. On the cliff above the park the houses leaned, blurred rectangles keeping watch.

Finally he took her elbow, turned her back to the car. In the steamy interior he made her take off her coat, her boots; dried her wet face with Kleenex. "Will you be all right now?" His voice was gentle.

She leaned against the upholstery, exhausted and drowsy in the sudden heat, and found herself smiling at the concern in his ice-flecked eyes. "Yes. Thank you." Uncaring suddenly, flushed and receptive, she was not surprised by the touch of his fingers on her face, running down her arm to her hand and back again. And she even welcomed the hard bite of his mouth, relaxed beneath it to slump against the solid heat of his body.

When she finally pulled herself away from him, he looked at his watch. "It's quarter to five. Everyone's left the office already. Shall we go back?"

He swung the car around, leaving the park to drive expertly through the slow-moving traffic. Back inside he nodded at the security guard; the elevator whirred. The deserted and darkened office hummed with quiet.

Judith hung up her coat and began clearing her still-cluttered desk, locking file cabinets. He poked his head out of his office. "Are you done?" Turning to face him, there was suddenly a spark of connection between them. Judith felt the strength of the afternoon in the warmth around the corners of his smile. "Come and look in here." She followed him into his office and over to the huge window. Below them the lights of the city were subdued under a filter of snow. They were so far above everything, disconnected and separate from that snarled and tangled conglomerate.

His hand touched her neck under her hair, gently moved her toward him until he blotted out the dotted lights below. Suddenly afraid, she fought against him in fierce but ineffectual silence. And then he was savage, bent her back and back in his persistence until she crumpled and fell, jarring against his desk. His hands, like his words, so blunt and direct. The rough surface of the carpet chafed under her naked legs and then she could no longer hold her resistance but joined him in the chill heat created by the afternoon.

As she scuffed down the hill to the barn, the wind billowed her open coat, pressed her shirt against her naked breasts, the cloth slippery ice on her nipples. Turning at the barn door to look at the house squatting at the top of the hill, she saw her path dark in the snow, a thin, steady chain linking the house to the barn. And the chain created by her and leading to her forged that strong connection. She saw her footsteps in perspective, a trail that she would wear through the snow all winter; a reference point, consistent.

She pushed open the barn door and the chill sheathing her skin submerged under the hazy warmth inside. The interior heat colliding with the cold air formed a pillow of steam that hung about her even after she pulled the door shut. She checked the thermometer in the plywood partitioned chorehouse: sixty degrees; the furnace worked.

Under the low-raftered ceiling the sows rose, yawning and scuffling, unprepared for her earliness. Blinking bleary orange eyes at the light, they sniffed and moaned with the stiffness of morning.

She collected the pails from the chorehouse and started to fill them with feed from the bin, the short scoop cold under her fingers. And suddenly felt hungry, as if the sharp air had somehow reinforced her body's demands. Oh well, there was plenty of time for breakfast. The pigs should be fed first now that they were awake.

A part of her consciousness heard a thin squeal; the sows rustled in their pens. Even with the water running, she could hear them shifting, edgy and impatient. The handle of the pail bit into her palm and she swung it down the aisle, water sloshing beside her. The pails were almost too heavy for her. Only with momentum and balance could she lift them over the fence to pour the water into the pigs' troughs.

He had never offered to help her and never

even seemed to notice when she struggled. Sometimes she ran behind the barn to pound her fists against the sides of her legs, crying with rage at his demands, his blindness to her inability to lift and carry, to swing like a muscular boy. But never told him, could never bring the words in her mouth out: I can't do it. Always tried, as stolid and stubborn as he was even as she refused to admit their similarity, herself and her father.

"Judy, aren't you done shoveling that load of feed yet?" And she gritted her teeth but said nothing and shoveled even more furiously.

Feed pails were always lighter, without the swing and pull that pails of water had: the water in control and almost flowing of its own accord, only allowing someone to guide the pail. A living thing as it mingled with the floury, brownish feed, satisfying the pigs more than chop alone ever would. The sows hated dry feed, insisted on water as small children at dinner do, whoofing at her for more, more.

Moving down the row of pens, she methodically shook a careful measure of chop into each trough: a quarter of a pail, four small shovelfuls each. Poured half a pail of water over it, the sow's head moving instantly to the trough to slurp and smack at the islands of feed. She bent over the fence of the last pen to empty the pail, then let it slide out of her hand and clatter against the cement floor.

The young sow lay rigid and shivering in her nest of straw, back pressed against the board fence. God, Judith thought, gripping the fence with both hands, what will I do, what will I do? I better call the vet right away. She bit her lip, fighting back tears, damn, damn, damn. If only she'd come out last night before she went to bed. What a fool not to check them. The sow drew a long, shuddering breath and released it with a spasmodic movement of pain, drawing her legs up against her belly. What should she tell the vet—convulsions? fever? Frozen, she clung to the fence, could not bring herself to climb it, all the hog diseases in her father's book repeating themselves in a chorus of panic, her ten beautiful sows lost.

So overwhelming was her anxiety that she didn't even notice the rustling in the straw behind the sow, a minuscule announcement for the smooth, tiny creature with bent ears and half-open eyes who staggered around his mother's legs uttering thin, desperate squeaks. A drying shred of placenta clung to his neck and the broken umbilical cord tangled bloody with his wobbling legs.

He ignored her completely, the woman leaning over the fence, unaware of himself as cause for the sudden amazement on her face. Until she started to laugh. It was the first sound he ever heard and he would remember it all his life—her laughter ringing in the endless space, in the brightness around him, in the musty smell and the sensation of air on his skin. He opened his eyes in amazement, but stumbling against the warmth of his mother's belly, recognized the laughter only as a herald of his arrival.

And she was laughing at herself, her fear and her own futility. Then suddenly quiet, she was watching him, his rushes at his mother's teats, nose just getting the smell of them before he slipped away. She stood there, undecided. Should she go into the pen? Would she upset the sow? Cautiously she slid over the fence, then leaned against it. It was the first time she had entered a pen aside from cleaning it. She took a small step forward and the sow raised her head with a defensive whoof. "It's okay," she said, coaxing softly. "It's only me, I won't hurt him. You know me, I'm Judith."

The sow rumbled in her throat and laid back her head, jerking her body against a further contraction. Under the whiteness of her swollen flank, ripples of movement flowed, then eased.

Murmuring quietly, "Come on, it's only me, relax," Judith squatted on her heels beside the sow, her voice strange and unfamiliar in the rustling stillness of the barn. She did not pick the tiny creature up but gently shoved him toward his mother, guided his snout to an engorged nipple. Under her hand she felt his back warm and silky. He opened his mouth wide and sucked loudly, hot milk down his throat in a wash of sweetness. She laughed again, softly this time. Eyes closed, he leaned back on her hand, bracing his legs against the straw-covered cement.

Squatting there beside him and the shivering, thrashing sow, she suddenly wanted to cry, overwhelmed by the terrible import of it. And looking up, she saw the other nine sows turned toward her, their heads resting on the edges of their fences, watching curious and silent. She supposed they were observing the newborn piglet but she should have known it was her just as much. After all, she had never spoken in the barn before, except for that one word last night. And now suddenly here she was talking and laughing—almost dancing in the aisle.

The sow moaned and grunted, cramped her body in a tight convulsive shudder, heaving. A crumpled snout pushed itself out of the raw and quivering gash, then a head and then the tiny, blood-smeared creature slid wriggling onto the straw.

"Judy, what's the matter?"

Almost reeling, she held tightly to the fence. She could hardly see over it, her chin resting on the top board. "They come out of her bum!" She was outraged, furious at him, hated her father and the groaning sow and the bloody piglet, kicked her feet against the fence and suddenly started to cry, anger catching at the sobs in her throat. He laid down the kicking piglet and came to her, standing her on the fence against him.

She struck at his chest with her small fists, not caring if she fell. "They come out of her bum!"

"Wait, wait." He held her tightly, imprisoning her hands. "They just come out of a hole that comes from her stomach. That's where they grow."

She stopped crying and looked at him doubtfully, his eyes so steady on her face. "How come?"

"I don't know," he said, his face serious. "They just do. You grew in your mother's stomach too."

"I didn't!" she said hotly, struggling against his arms like a captive bird. "I did not!"

He swung her down to the floor inside the pen with him. "Just a minute, Judy."

She was crying again, knuckling at her eyes so that he had to touch her to make her look. In the cup of his two rough hands he held the piglet, shining silky and white, beady black eyes blinking at the warmth around him. "Look," he said softly, "just look."

She stared at the newborn piglet, sulky and blinking tears from her eyes. Involuntarily her hand stole out, her finger reached to touch the edge of his almost-transparent ear . . . She pulled her hand back and put it behind her.

"You can touch him," he said.

She shook her head, stubborn.

"Come on. Isn't he little? Look what a nice nose he has."

And then she could not control her hand

edging cautiously toward him, touched his back gingerly to feel the warm vibrancy of him and then the delicate sheen of his ear, her fingers thrilling with the alive pulse of him. He sneezed suddenly and she jumped back, wide-eyed.

Her father laughed and put the pig down, lifted her over the fence again. "He'll grow almost as big as you, Judy-girl."

"He's soft," she said. "Can I name him?"

"Well, you won't be able to tell the difference between him and all his brothers and sisters."

"It doesn't matter," she said. "I'll call him, ummm, Sammy."

He laughed. "Okay. You better go inside now."

She hung on the fence. "Can't I stay here?"

"Do you want to?"

She nodded seriously.

"Well, then you've got to be quiet or you'll upset the mother."

Now she bent quickly to the second piglet, the feel of him slimy and wet under her hand. Prying open his mouth, she cleared the mucus out with her finger, wiped his tiny snout and rubbed him with a handful of straw until he started to gasp. She smelled him warm and pungent like a clod of freshly overturned earth. In the next moment he was wriggling to get his unsteady feet beneath him.

She sat back, rubbing rough straw between her hands. "Two," she said gleefully, and the sow in the next pen whoofed softly. Together they watched his efforts to stand. He was shivery and smaller than the firstborn but he was soon staggering about. She estimated that the first one was probably at least half an hour older, dry and already walking when she first saw him. It reminded her. "Hey," she said to the interested sow in the next pen. "What's the matter with me?" I'd better get a heat lamp, she thought, so these little guys can dry off and keep warm. Gently she put the new piglet close to its mother, then slipped over the fence and ran from the barn to the house, her big boots sliding on the snow up the hill.

Her tracks lay half-erased by snowflakes and she destroyed what was left of their neat precision in her stumbling race to the house. But she slowed at the top of the hill, the shimmering stillness around her penetrating her haste and excitement. The snow had stopped falling and a late-rising sun glittered the soft whiteness to icy blue. She stood still, looking around her glowing world: the white, self-effacing house, the vibrant red barn, the jeweled celebration of the snow.

Carefully she walked to a smooth patch, flopped down on her back and swung her arms through the snow high above her head and down to her sides, then spread her legs and brought them together, again and again in a convulsive act of love. Finally standing, back covered with snow, she jumped clear of the angel then turned and dashed to the house. Inside, she ran to the closet where she kept the heat lamps. She took a lamp and carried it carefully, cradling it in her arms, six dollars for just one.

In her hurry to get back to the warmth and light of the barn, she hardly noticed the morning grayness of the house. Holding the big lamp gingerly, she smiled at her angel imprint, hurried back down the hill sliding on the soles of her boots. She jerked open the barn door, then forced herself to stay quiet as she walked down the aisle to the pen.

"Here I am again," she said. "It only took a minute."

They swung their heads to follow her movement to the end of the row. She had words, a voice! Her laughter echoed in their bristly, perked-up ears like a remembrance of things past. She had returned, the woman who took them, who had chosen them so carefully. She had roused herself out of that sour-smelling, silent human who had kept them for a month. They rustled with joy and satisfaction at her, Judith.

He had waited until the next afternoon to talk to her.

"Can you come into my office for a moment, please?" Having studiously ignored and avoided her all morning.

She rose and walked around her desk away from the safety of the typewriter, the dress clinging to her hips. He shut the door, motioned her to sit down, went to stand behind the shield of his own desk.

He cleared his throat, a white edge around his mouth. "Judith, I don't quite know what to say . . ."

She interrupted him fiercely. "Don't say anything."

Surprised, he looked at her and waited. When she said nothing more he gathered himself and went on. "You have a right to be pretty upset with me after last night."

She felt he was trying to deny the whole afternoon, the snow, that sudden flash of understanding between them; and suddenly angrier than she could ever remember, she rose and took a step toward him, her voice low and tight. "When are you damned men going to stop being so egotistical? I don't suppose the idea has entered your head that if I hadn't wanted to be seduced, I wouldn't have let you. And if you must apologize for everything you do, why do you bother doing it at all?"

He stood, taken aback, offense gathering on his face.

"And," she added quickly, "I'll tender my resignation this afternoon."

He studied her, puzzlement overtaking his surprise. Then understanding, he laughed shortly, eyes hard and determined. "I see. And if I don't apologize, you won't resign."

"You're right." She leaned against the desk and waited, her anger ebbing to uncertainty.

He walked to the door, locked it and came back and stood in front of her. She looked up at him steadily.

"Okay?" he asked. It was not a question. His hands on her shoulders were heavy and strong. Under their weight she felt her back pressed against the edge of the desk, her legs balancing her body precariously. Sliding her skirt up, she felt him move against her, his aggression holding her pivoted.

And now there were piglets in the barn. Their inexperienced but expectant bodies sensed the birth; instinctively they recognized the sound and passage of it. It was an event: their own bellies tightened with it, with anticipation. And behind the door, beyond the windows, they smelled the fresh snow. Its crystal fragrance hung in the air like the sharp smell of a boar. It permeated everything, lifted their noses and tails with eagerness. She carried it too; she was soaked in it, a colorless aura of chill sexuality that dissipated around her in the warmth of the barn.

When she reached the last pen there were two more wet and shivering piglets. Gently she rubbed them with straw, then screwed the heat lamp into the hanging socket that dangled from the ceiling over the small enclosure boarded off at the end of the pen. Taking a packet of straw from the bale by the chorehouse, she arranged it under the glowing red lamp, then shoved them under the warmth. They squealed, protesting feebly when she picked them up; but under the lamp they stopped shivering and the youngest of them promptly fell asleep on the straw. The partition protected the lamp from their mother, the bottom board removed and leaving a space for them to get in and out of the nest. The straw formed a thick shield in front of the opening but the two oldest burrowed through it and staggered back to their mother. For them, eating was better than sleeping.

Judith laughed at their determination, put some straw in a corner of the pen and sat down on it to wait, her feet stretched in front of her.

The sow moaned and the next pig flopped out in a rush of blood, still inside the gray placenta. Judith ripped open the sack, shuddering at the slimy mass under her hands, and pulled the pig free. Boneless and unmoving, it lay perfectly still. She opened the unresisting jaws and cleared phlegm from the mouth and nose, rubbing the limp piglet vigorously with straw. It lay waxy and relaxed in a paradox of sleep.

"Not a dead one already," she said. Frantic, she picked it up by two tiny, slippery hind feet and slapped at the ribbed sides until the piglet heaved a gasp and started to wriggle in her hand. Sighing with relief, Judith put her under the lamp where she stumbled about over the other sleeping piglets until they awoke, then squeaked until she scrambled out of the straw nest and found her way to her mother.

Judith laughed at her, the smallest of them, so pugnacious. "You little tough," she said. "Stepped all over your brothers, did you?"

Always from over the fence Judy watched them, the new pigs come alive, slip out of their mother's hole, stagger up out of inertia and darkness into movement and light. She never dared to climb into the pen but watched for their sneeze, their stumbling efforts to walk. If one of them didn't move she ran for her father, for his big hands to bring them to life. And then the very tiny pig, he must be a runt, lay so perfectly still. "Daddy, Daddy!" But he wasn't there, didn't answer her. "Daddy, daddy, where are you?" She ran back into the barn, the piglet lying as still as death, and she could hardly scramble over the fence, her legs not long enough to reach. She rubbed him with a handful of straw, as she had seen her father do so often, but he lay limp, refusing to move. Crying, she hit him with her small fist, struck at his feeble ribs furiously. "Don't die, don't die." And suddenly he opened his tiny mouth and gasped faintly. Trembling, she picked him up and held him wet against her red coat to carry him to the heat lamp, stepping carefully over the partition to put him down.

"Is he okay?" Her father's big boots came down the aisle to the pen.

"Yes," she said, smearing the blood on her coat with her arm. "I made him breathe."

He swung over the fence and looked down at the runt, still gasping under the lamp. "You sure did." He lifted her to the top of the fence. "I'll stay here and watch now."

She looked at him, her face level with his. "I could watch."

Laughing at her serious face, he held her on the fence in her red coat and small black boots, stroking her hair with his rough hand.

Judith wheeled the barrow in front of the pen and forked the wet straw from around the stretched-out, now-sleeping sow, then scooped up the slippery mound of afterbirth with the shovel. Now there were eleven of them scuffling and squeaking around the sow. She overturned the barrow on the snowy manure heap, covered the wet, bloody straw with snow, then hurried back into the warm haven of the barn. Inside again, she scattered fresh, clean straw around the pen and the mother, around the wriggling row of eleven rigid and eager backs.

The sow jerked impatiently at the sharp teeth on her swollen teats, and Judith went to the chorehouse to get the tooth clipper. It felt familiar, the handles under her fingers opening and closing the clamp, the instrument shaped like a tiny wire cutter. Wondered if she could still do it easily and effortlessly. She slid her legs over the fence and picked up one of the piglets, held him too tightly so that he wriggled and squealed. She almost dropped him; put him back down. "Shit."

She held the clipper in her right hand, manipulating it, then picked up another piglet, her fingers nervous and awkward. He squealed and struggled too, but she held him, fingers tight around the back of his neck behind his ears. Then she could not move the clipper to clamp his tiny, curved teeth. She put him down again, clenched her fist. "Damn."

Angry at herself, she picked him up once more and suddenly it was easy, the movements of the simple operation coming back to her hands. She edged the clipper in under the curl of his lip, baring his gum; clamped it on the tiny, sharp tooth, breaking it with a small, precise snap.

Her father would hold the piglets while she stood, the clipper awkward in her fingers, afraid to hear the snap of teeth. "Come on, Judy. Look, it's easy." Taking the clipper from her, he snapped the teeth as easily as a toothpick, his hands quick and sure. "Okay, now you do it." He picked up another pig for her.

"But I'm scared I'll pinch his tongue."

"Look." Putting down the pig, he shaped

her fingers around the handles. "Hold it like this, see, then you can move the handles easily. Now pick up the pig, hold him by the back of his neck behind his ears and you'll keep his head still at the same time." Guiding her hands, he snapped the teeth quickly. "Okay, now you do it yourself."

She held the small cutter carefully and picked up the pig. Slowly, oh so slowly, she edged the clipper beside his tongue, clamped the tiny fangs, snapped.

"That's right. See, it's easy."

Two fangs on each side, upper and lower, she broke them out in succession: lower left, upper left, lower right, upper right, leaving small ragged holes where the teeth had been, a tiny center of blood. One by one she picked them up and broke out their teeth, the second easier than the first, the third easier than the second. It came back effortlessly even though they struggled and squealed indignantly, angry at the intrusion on their comfort.

The sows stood and whoofed at their cries. The mother, anxious and protective, grunted angrily and struggled to get up.

In a few moments she was finished. "Whew, for a minute there I thought I'd forgotten how." She wiped white splinters of teeth off the clipper with a bit of straw, rubbed her hands on the sides of her jeans. "Sorry, Mum, but they'll hurt you if I don't do it." The sow whoofed in reply. Judith bent down and scratched behind her ear. "Hey, come on, we've done great today—eleven babies and all of them alive and well." The impatient sow snorted as if to say that she had done all the work.

"Sure, I know, but remember, we're in this together. Me and you. The pigs and Judith Pierce."

She frowned, hesitated. "That won't do. If

this is a partnership, you have to have a share. A name." She laughed suddenly. "That's it, I'll christen you!" She scrambled out of the pen and flew to the chorehouse, ran some water into a pail and then carried it back to the last pen. Sprinkling it on the sow's head she said, "In the name of hogs, farming and hog farming, I hereby christen you . . . umm . . . Marie Antoinette! What the heck, you're better than royalty." The sow shook her head, making the droplets fly. "Marie Antoinette," she repeated, bending down to scratch behind her large, bristly ears. "And I hereby state that on the day that you give birth to your first piglets, every one of you will be given a name and public recognition in this enterprise."

They grunted at her excited voice, joining with their own deep-throated cries. The bravest sow at the front put her delicate white forelegs on the top board of her fence and stood upright to lead the chorus, even the newborn piglets joining with their squeals. Judith felt happiness from a place inside her that she had almost forgotten about.

Finally she trudged up the hill to the house, grateful for the cooling snow that seemed to rest her eyes and ease her suddenly stiff and aching back. Her stomach rumbled; she had forgotten all about breakfast and it was almost lunchtime now.

She dropped her coat and boots in a heap by the door, oddly relieved to escape the brilliance outside. Moving slowly about the kitchen, she made herself an enormous breakfast, bacon and eggs and toast, and ate it slowly, abstractedly, sitting at the kitchen table and looking out at the snow-covered yard. Beyond the window and removed from her, even the angel was unconnected to anything in the morning.

Judith would have been at work for hours

already, typing the morning's letters, opening the mail, answering the telephone. By noon the artificial taste of cigarettes in her mouth made her want to scrub her teeth, running her tongue over the thin scum on them, to drink water, to retch. Instead she lit another and saw herself, a picture through her father's eyes: cigarette, blue eye-shadow, fingernails long and glossy with scarlet polish. She cringed, huddled lower on her typist's stool, the gray typewriter keys blurred. But you don't have to see to type. Just keep the fingers moving, don't stop, read the polysyllabic words beside you as fast as you can and your fingers should keep going, keep typing automatically, your fingers reading the words while eyes blur unfocused. A good secretary can . . . keep going.

She turned her back on the window, put her plate in the sink and walked away, through the living room to the closeness of her bedroom. She stripped off the shirt and blue jeans and heavy socks, threw them in a heap on the floor. She crawled into bed, naked and shivering, to fall asleep, letting the whole day slip away unnoticed.

Six

Now she always woke automatically, immediately honed for the day. And it was not the morning edging in on her eyelids and the swirl of cold air through the open window, but the thought of them that roused her. Ridiculous, of course—they didn't need her; they had Marie Antoinette. When the opening barn door awakened them, they snuffled out of their straw nest to nuzzle their mother, feeling almost iridescent with warmth and life, rubbing against the rough bristles of her hide, feeling the smoothness of her nipples on their tongues.

She always came to lean over the fence and watch them, talking softly, her voice rising and falling in the murmuring air. She passed it off, her sudden change, as pride of ownership. At least, after resisting for so long, she had the grace to be embarrassed. They seemed so brilliant to her in contrast to the surrounding winter gray. Making quick, dazzling rushes on skittering legs, they surveyed her with darting black eyes, a mischievous cockiness that made her laugh.

Small, square hands on the top board of the fence, Judy always watched, eyes round. They played for her, the piglets dashing and squealing until she smiled. She watched them passionately, with a boundless fascination, until her father came to get her. "Time to go inside now, Judy, come on." With her hand in his she turned away, still looking over her shoulder at their curious and upturned pigfaces.

And now she lagged over her chores as if searching for an excuse to stay in the barn longer; she rummaged and picked up in an excess of tidiness.

The change, her new eagerness, made them restless. They waited for her to change again, even as they savored their stability, the food, the warmth, the clean, snow-smelling straw from the stack in front of the barn.

The snow stopped, fell again, then covered a few days of stillness. It seemed molded, the world suppressed under whiteness. And then the snow fell once more but no longer still and muffling. The wind orchestrated it into drifts and patterns all down the tree-lined driveway and swept the hill between the house and the barn with dunes.

Under a low and sullen morning sky Judith bent her head against the wind, then went back inside to wrap a scarf around her neck. She cleared the sidewalk to the house then stamped a path to the barn through the whipped mounds to find a perfectly molded ridge resting against the door, sealing the barn against intrusion.

She ran back to the house and returned with a shovel, her toes already numbing. She attacked the drift vigorously, heaving the snow into a pile over her shoulder and erasing her body into the movement's form: bend, scoop, straighten, fling; bend, scoop, straighten, fling . . .

At breakfast Judy's mother turned the dial of the radio.

"All schools in the county of Stettler will be closed today due to blowing snow and bad weather conditions. Repeat: Buses in the county of Stettler will not be running today. All schools are closed . . ."

Judy stirred sugar into her bowl. "Goodie!"

Her father swallowed great spoonfuls of porridge. "You can shovel snow for me today, Judy."

Beyond the barn door, they heard the sound and felt the fixed rhythm of her shoveling. Swinging her body, swiveling, she felt a slow edge of energy take over from the sluggishness of her bones. She could feel them again, brittle and sharp. That same sensation going home to the farm on the dayliner, so painful the press of her bones. Sitting tense on the upholstered seat, hands not holding a cigarette but curled in on each other, awkward with the waiting. Aware of a hollow catch in her breath when she inhaled the train smell of dust and old shoes, of half-eaten bananas.

It would be the three of them again, mother and father and Judy. They would be wondering, but afraid to ask. Afraid to ask the right questions. Every trip from the city the same, the old coach stopping and starting at deserted stations on the edges of decaying towns. She sat with her feet tight on the tiled floor, only her head bent to watch the movement beyond the window. The train rocked heavily, galloped from the open space around the city suburbs to clusters of small towns, then crept into the Battle River valley along a creek entrance. Paralyzed with waiting, she could still lean her elbow on the dusty sill and watch the evergreen branches flicker past, slumped under a weight of snow. This was the best part of the trip, humming between trees along the south side of the river valley. Funny, the south side was always covered with trees, protected; the north side bare and exposed. Exposed. Like her face, open and raw, inviting intrusion. And how to evade them, their eyes on her face always questioning, trying to read her eyes, the set of her mouth.

"No," she said. "I can't come back and

live here." And she tried to say it scornfully, even while she felt the edge of something bitter rising at the back of her throat.

They were silent, the lines around their eyes and mouths etched gray and harsh under the bright florescence of the kitchen light. She saw them from a great distance as if they were fading away, watched them as curiously as if they were unconnected to her. She hardly heard her mother's querulous voice rising and drifting. Under the light the shadow falling across her father's face was still as death.

"We have to sell it then, Judy-girl." His hands hung open and useless between his knees; head down, he refused even to look at her. "We just wanted to ask you first, give you a chance."

Gripping her hands tight as fists together in her lap she could feel the chilling stillness in him. "But why, Daddy? Can't you wait just a little longer?"

"I'm too old." The words were his flat admission of defeat, that the dust and the cold and the heat and the pigs and the long days had finally penetrated to his thick, bent frame.

She wanted to reach to him and put her arms around him with the same childlike faith she had carried all this time; but thought of coming back, here, and something inside her shuddered at the knowledge of the grinding days. "I can't," she cried. "I just can't. Don't you see, it's here, this place, the life, all the women are housewives and all the men are country louts. The only thing to do is go to pot-luck suppers and Elks' dances. Every day is the same. I hate it, I hate it, I want to do things, can't you understand?"

His blue eyes were faded, not so bright as she remembered them. "But those things don't matter, Judy, if you have the farm, if you've got animals and things to do, and you build."

Her mother started to cry. "You just don't care." But he only sat there, silent and unspeaking, refusing to try to persuade her, refusing even to look at her again.

The train swung around a long curve and she jolted against the side of the seat. She remembered his fingers this afternoon on the small of her back, easing against her, and then the circular pattern of the room strange and upside-down from the carpeted floor. "Give it up," she told herself, "give it up." It was the question she knew they would ask her for the last time in the kitchen that night, the three of them sitting around the table in an attitude of togetherness. She answered it already, "No, no," the flavor of her self-abnegation tasting sweet in her mouth, her delicious abasement. And she was only a spectator at the window of the swaying train, no connection to the escaping landscape.

At the barn door she hesitated for a moment. The drift was diminished to a pile of crumpled snow. Touching the icy handle gingerly, she tugged the door open against the resistance of the remaining snow and quickly pulled it shut behind her.

In the cobweb breath of the barn they could sense her relief at being out of the relentless snow. Here waited only the pungent shadows of their daily ritual, soothing and indifferent. She turned on the lights and called to them, answered the grunts and whoofs as she walked down the aisle between the pens. Her voice, soft as it was, cut through the pig-laden air of the barn. She went to the back to check the new piglets, stood for a moment watching them clamped to their mother's teats, then turned and went back to the second pen.

Hands in her pockets and shoulders still hunched, she stood watching the sow inside the pen. The sow ignored her, tossing straw in her mouth to shape a careful nest in the corner. Suddenly aware, she turned and whoofed at Judith, grinding her teeth. She gnawed the board fence, rooted at its implacable surface holding her captive, then went back to pawing her straw nest.

"So you're going to have pigs today," Judith said, straightening her body and tipping her head back. "Do the rest of you think I'm right?"

She looked at them, heads alert and waiting at the sound of her voice. "Well, I guess that's some kind of agreement."

And although she pretended to be calm and nonchalant while she scooped feed and poured water into the troughs, she worked impatiently, almost jerkily, a queer, excited smile on her face.

"Josephine," she said, tossing a chunk of fresh straw into the sow's pen. "You'll be Josephine from now on."

Ignoring her mash, Josephine kept on nudging restlessly at her nest. "I'll be back soon," Judith said, slamming the door behind her.

In the house she ate breakfast hungrily, impatient with her body for its demands. Clearing the drift had taken longer than she thought it would; it was late. She went to the closet for a heat lamp, then pulled on an extra pair of socks; her feet still felt like cold lumps of lead after the morning's shoveling.

Almost out the door, she heard a car drive into the yard, its engine whirring above the wind. "Damn."

Without waiting to find out who it was, she tugged on her boots. She was going to the barn anyway. But when she jerked open the door to the quiet knock, she found Mina standing huddled against the wind on the doorstep. Her navy duffel coat was sprinkled with snow. "Judith?"

Just so her mother had stood, one hand

holding the door open, the other bunching the top of her cardigan together. "It means so much to him." Her mother's eyes, narrowed against the blazing snow, were abstracted, patient with her inevitable pleading. "Can't you just think about it a little more, Judith?"

Her mother calling her Judith for the first time, as if she had grown up, was suddenly and inexplicably adult. And because of that she hesitated momentarily, standing in the cold morning on the doorstep she had tread so long, all her years as a child. Facing her mother there in the doorway, huddled against the draft, she wished she could stay Judy, Judy forever.

"Yes," she said wearily, turning away from her mother's relentless eyes, "I'll think about it, but I don't think I'll change my mind." And she walked quickly through the snow to the car, knowing her father would say nothing, would not even wave when the train pulled away.

"Are you busy today?" Mina asked.

She gestured impatiently toward the barn. "One of my sows is coming in. I have to watch her."

"Well." Mina waved at the car. "Ed and Jim are going to town, why on earth in the middle of a blizzard I don't know. Anyway, I didn't feel like sitting at home, so I thought I would come over and keep you company. Maybe you'd have some stuff to clean up in the house I could help with, but if I'd be in the way . . ."

"Oh, no," Judith interrupted, surprised at her own quickness. She didn't really want to have anyone else there while the sow had piglets. But she heard herself saying, "Please stay—as long as you don't mind coming to the barn with me and sitting there." Damn, why was she so polite?

Mina laughed. "Not in the least. I'd like to." She ran to the car and shouted through the window, "You can pick me up when you get back."

Watching them, she heard Jim say to Mina, "Ask her when she's coming over again." Then the car slid away, a spume of snow spraying from the sides as the wheels cut through the drifts.

"Your driveway will be completely snowed in pretty soon," Mina observed. "Better ask Ed to clear it out a little with the bucket."

"It doesn't matter."

"Huh, it will when you want to get out, or when the feed truck wants to get in. Unless you don't want either."

She had to smile at the big glasses perched on the small, serious face under the blue hood. "You're so practical."

"I have to be. No one else is at our house."

"No one?"

Mina laughed, shrugged, a quick movement of fragile bones that somewhat emphasized the brownness of her hair and face. Only the big glasses were foreign, disguising her eyes.

One behind the other, they walked down the hill to the barn, Judith holding the heat lamp close against her chest with a mittened hand.

And opening the door, she was conscious of a swift sense of proprietorship. This was her barn and these were her pigs. She was as proud as some women are of their houses, of the nests they create around their men and family.

The pigs heard them coming, heard voices, the barn door opening; knew there was someone else with her. So when the two women came in, they were whoofing and grunting, sows' heads thrust over the boards to smell, ears twitched forward, seeing the roughness of the strange woman's coat and her short, fragile body.

"It's okay, settle down there, it's a friend."

Judith's firm, quiet voice penetrated their noise and gradually quieted them until only the new mother snorted and rumbled her protection.

Mina sat down on an overturned pail to watch. Judith eased into Josephine's pen, talking softly, constantly, while she hung the lamp in place and moved the feed trough out of the way. She wasn't afraid like the last time, only concerned. But it was more than that, almost as if she was performing or showing off—"See, look at this!" And over everything, the pigs breathed the sharp female smell of them mixed together, indistinguishable but still two separate smells, both of them there alone but mingling.

Judith slid her legs over the fence and pulled a straw bale into the aisle to sit on. "Well, we can just wait. She'll settle down pretty soon."

"You really do like it, don't you?" Mina asked.

Judith blushed then nodded almost defensively. "Yes, I guess I do."

"It helps." Then quickly, aware of the reaction, Mina said, "I'm not making fun of you."

"Well . . ." Judith spoke slowly, with difficulty. She hadn't exposed herself for so long, and to a woman yet. "I'm not always sure if I do like it."

Mina nodded. "It can't be perfect all of the time. Seems to me you've done pretty good getting this far. It means it's more than just a whim for you."

She shrugged, unwilling to commit herself. "Maybe I don't have any choice."

"Maybe that's what you tell yourself." Mina watched her closely. "You must have picked this over something else."

"Sometimes I don't know." She heard her voice in her ears as if from a great distance, projected from something beyond and outside her. "It's as if something else made me do it. I didn't really want to, but I had to. It was some other person directing and I was just carrying out orders."

"Don't give yourself any credit, heh? Pretty sensible orders by the looks of it," Mina said dryly.

Judith turned away, still humorless, still unable to expose herself. "Tell me about you," she said.

Mina made a face. "Who me? I'm married and over forty with three sons and a husband. I'm more or less free to be happy."

"Is that all?"

Mina wanted her to laugh, to relieve that sense of vulnerability. She spread her hands. "What else is there to say about forty-year-old farm wives. I live in a four-bedroom, ranch-style house on the south half of Section 31, Township X, Range 9, west of the fifth meridian. Hell, I can never get the land description right. Wife of owner. Dower rights on the home quarter."

"Dower rights on the home quarter," Judith repeated seriously. Mina's quick self-negation puzzled her. "Is that how you think of yourself?"

Mina burst out laughing, shaking cobwebs in the corners of the barn.

Yes, yes, the pigs knew it was what Judith needed—laughter, laughter echoing around her. If they could have laughed, they would have joined in.

Mina subsided. "To myself I'm a petite and interesting woman who has a secret vivacity and sense of beauty that no great person has discovered yet. I'm just waiting for that to happen and I can leave the south half of Section 31 behind." She sat quietly for a moment, looking down at her hands. "Daydreams. Of course it never will."

Judith could not help her amazement at Mina's openness, her seeeming invulnerability.

"How can you be so . . . ?" She hesitated, looking for the right word, wondering what she really meant.

Mina laughed again. "Hey, do you ever read books?"

"Not very much. I used to read novels when I lived in the city."

"Well, reading books has convinced me that even the smallest thing I do is important. So there."

Judith shook her head, uncomprehending.

"You lived in the city," Mina said.

"Yeah."

Instantly it returned, the irrepressible movement inside of her to leave everything, leave the pigs and go back, Judith running to meet him, to release herself, feeling the surprising strength of his hands and arms, the quick and sudden energy of her own body in their movement together. It was the slaking of that sensuality she had ached with, running in the pasture at night, whipping through the thigh-high grass to dispel her body's restlessness. Sometimes she couldn't even think of his name. Not that it mattered; it was the act, the pleasure, that was important. And yet she recoiled from it, the brutality of it. Far better to be here on a straw bale with a slightly batty neighbor lady.

"Lucky," said Mina. "You know what it's really like. I've never lived in the city."

Turning to Mina, Judith forced herself to push back the insistence of the past, that nagging sense of physical loss. "You grew up around here?"

"Not around here, but close—in Rosewood. No roses either, by the way."

"You got married right away?"

"More or less. I finished high school, wanted to study French literature but Ed was there, and you know . . ." She shrugged.

"Yes." She played absentmindedly with a straw, twisting it between her fingers.

Norman leaning against her, she was paralyzed by his weight, his insistence. "Look, Judy, we'll get married. It'll be so much better than this fooling around and waiting until we're older."

She wavered under his pressure like a reed, but even then held her determination—no, no, not this man, so stiff, so tight. "No, we can't."

"If you go away to work in the city, you'll never come back, Judy. You'll forget about me."

"Don't be silly. Of course I can't forget about you." She refused to look at his face.

"But Judy . . ."

"Look, Mom and Dad want me to go and work in the city for a while. They want me to be sure before I start farming. I'll be back." Holding her breath against the lie, almost wanting to cross her fingers trapped inside his sweaty palms.

"Why did you get married then?" She asked Mina lazily, knowing the demands of the question.

Mina spread her hands. "What could I do, he had a gun!" Her laughter freed itself, lost that tinge of regret. "Same thing happen to you?"

"No. I went to the city and took a secretarial course and worked . . ."

"But almost the same," Mina said.

"I'm not married."

"Doesn't matter. They all get us sooner or later."

"How do you mean?"

"You're back on the farm, aren't you? You're here because some man did something to you. Maybe good, maybe bad. Maybe your father or your brother or some other guy. You don't do anything like this without a reason."

Judith tried to laugh but it was unconvincing. "For myself."

"Maybe, but other people help to push you into it. I have a feeling that what you say is true, that you're not sure if you really like it, but you're giving it a try."

"You're contradicting yourself. This is just my way of making a living."

Mina laughed again. "I always contradict myself—it's my way of figuring things out."

"So, then what do you figure?" Judith asked the question dryly, defensive, trying to silence her.

Mina looked directly at her for a long moment. "Maybe we could get along okay," she said finally, the words coming slowly and carefully.

Trapped, she had to look at Mina, the direct eyes behind the glasses, the almost childish mouth under her straight nose.

In the barn there was a shivering silence; only the rustling of straw and the movement of the wind outside audible. They stayed silent, facing each other—the small, brown woman muffled in a too-large coat and the other in thick sweater and blue jeans. Heads cocked, the pigs were silent. Judith passed a nervous hand through her hair.

After a long moment she jumped up and clambered over the fence, kneeling beside the shuddering sow. "I knew it," she said, "the first pig." She rubbed it with straw, busily covering her confusion with movement. Mina did not stir but sat watching her calmly.

When the pig was safely under the heat lamp, Judith slid over the board fence again, bent to scrub her bloody hands with straw. She hesitated, then blindly thrust her right hand toward Mina. Eyes following relentlessly, the pigs saw Mina get to her feet, take Judith's hand in both her own and hold it there, the two of them caught together in the incantation of their joining.

Seven

Within her room she slept and woke and slept and woke. Turning on her back to face the sloping ceiling in the mornings she was lulled, enclosed, the hard narrow bed beneath her as constant as her sleep in the city had never been. This room was hers, separate from the others. When she thought of the brightness of her mother's house, that house where everything carried a sheen, polished and polished again, this house was small and gray, this room the only one that held a snatch of her breath in it.

But at least it was hers. Hers to leave unpolished and without definition. Except for this bedroom, where the smell of her sleep hung faint and musky in the air.

She had papered the walls with leftover wallpaper from Eaton's basement, a slate-gray background randomly sprinkled with Oriental-looking butterflies. It was cheap and gaudy but an instantaneous collusion when she discovered it, some madness making her take it, purchasing a fragment of the past at the rouged cashier's desk. She covered the walls with it, carrying the long, dripping strips of paper from the bathroom to the bedroom, struggling up the stepladder and making elaborate efforts to smooth out the wrinkles. Even so, the edges did not quite match; there was a thin gap where the pink paint of the former owner showed through.

The butterflies. Papering her own room in

her own house on her own pig farm with that wallpaper—it might have been an admission.

"That," she said in the material store, tugging at her mother's arm while her mother looked at serviceable green and blue cottons and linens. She reached to feel it, the grain of cloth between her fingers easily crushed.

"Judy, it's such thin and flimsy material. It's no good for school."

"But for Sunday," she whispered frantically. "For Sunday. Please, oh please, it's so beautiful."

Her mother shook her head. "But you need a school dress, Judy."

She could not tear her eyes from the bolt. "Please, oh please." The butterflies floated apricot and green before her senses, exotic orchids that would surround her in undiscovered mysteries. They were sheared from the bolt by an impatient clerk, with her mother still shaking her head as she separated tightly folded dollars from her wallet.

And when she wore it she was beyond the world, beyond everything.

"This is my little girl, Judy." Holding tightly to the thickness of his hand, she was shy and diffident, wanting to draw back when he pushed her forward.

"What a pretty name." The tall man leaned down to take her hand. The pants of his suit were so sharply creased she shuddered. Her father's suits were worn and shapeless; he had only two. "And what a pretty little girl you are. I never imagined farm girls were so pretty."

Judy scuffed her toe in the dust.

"And will you be a farmer's wife?"

She looked up at her father. "No, I'm going to work for Daddy."

The city man laughed. "Of course."

Her father's hand was warm and heavy on her shoulder.

"She doesn't look like you," the man said to her father.

She sidled away as quickly as they let her go, slipped out of the house to run, the skirt of the orange dress sticking to her legs, pressing between them in the wind. When she twirled, the dress spun itself out around her, apricot butterflies floating alive and prickly, the pattern of their distortion shaping them perverse and fantastical, repeating itself imperfectly on the silky surface.

Judith wished she had found the butterfly wallpaper in the city and celebrated her apartment with it. It would have been a change from the yellowish walls and white ceiling. The slate background would have matched the slate of his eyes, cool and piercing, the directness that she first welcomed and then learned to evade, twist herself around. The butterflies might have widened for her to disappear into, and she would not have been his vortex, she would not have felt him expecting her to widen indefinitely and forever.

Her room, butterflies and all. Under the cool slip of the sheet, she ran her hands in circles over her breasts, her belly, her hips, down to her thighs and up again, parting herself, opening to the intrusion of her own fingers. Their narrowness was insubstantial and unsatisfying, her widening cleft wanted a pushing bluntness to engorge it, chafe its tender scarlet wetness swollen until it had to convulse, tighten unbearably under the stroke of that relentlessly voluptuous attack.

She longed for the solidity of his body to roll over against and take inside her. She ached with that lost fulfillment, hand still caressing her open thighs, repeating and repeating, the inflexible rhythm of her own dry pleasure emphasizing her lonely dissatisfaction.

Even Norman was better. The car lights dying until the tangle of brush and weeds at the end of the deserted lane vanished into darkness. She felt his arms closing on her like a vise. Even resisting she felt herself give in—the insistence of his mouth, his palms, his body pressed too close to hers. Felt herself quicken as she denied him, groping, fumbling at her, crumpling the cloth of her dress under damp palms.

And yet she was detached, almost cruel. She refused to touch him, produced indignation at his furtive plea, so that he brought himself, hand pumping in the shadowed interior of the car. And then, skirt bunched around her waist, guided his fingers inside her, desperate for something more than her own, willing to allow him even this small victory.

"Judy, am I hurting you?"

Refusing to answer him, she forced his clumsy too-careful fingers into her, pushed herself over them, aching for slow clean strokes instead of his feeble bungling, his awkwardness so irritating that finally she drew away from him, blind with anger.

He was wide-eyed, anxious. "Did it break?"

She had a savage desire to pound at him with her fists, to claw his face. What, you clumsy fool? What are you talking about? You must be crazy. I've played with myself for so long I can't remember. Do you think I've kept myself for you to botch with your stupid fingers? But said nothing, would not even look at him.

In scornful silence she smoothed the wrinkled skirt of her dress, ignoring the anxiety in his eyes, his fearful waiting. Until finally she said, "It's eleven o'clock. You better get me home."

And driving home she could watch the transformation, what he convinced himself was his triumph overrunning his apprehension. In the green light from the dashboard his lips were tilted in a smile of possession. And she even let him believe it, so futile she wished only to be alone in the nimbus before sleep, never to see or speak to him again. Wish I'd never let him touch me, she thought. Idiot.

Judith rolled onto her stomach, turning her face on the pillow to let the muted winter light filter through her half-closed eyes. She thought of the pigs and then of the cold outside, eased her body deeper into the cocoon of her nest, falling into a light sleep even as she told herself to get up, eat breakfast, go to the barn. And woke to mid-morning sunshine, rigid and startled as if by a sudden noise.

The house held itself secret and still as she lay listening, completely awake. Then she heard it again, someone pounding on the door beyond the living room and kitchen, someone who knew by the truck that she was home.

She sprang out of bed and scrambled into jeans and a shirt, shaking her head to clear the remnants of sleep. Barefoot on the cold linoleum, she hurried through the house to the door, pulling it open to let in a swirling draft of icy wind.

Just walking away, Jim Stamby turned back at the sound of the door. He grinned. "There you are. Hey, I thought you were dead or something."

"No," she said stupidly. "I'm okay."

"I knocked and knocked and you didn't answer, so I went down to the barn but you weren't there. I figured maybe you were hiding on me or you were sick." Beyond his shoulder she saw the black-and-white flash of a magpie. "I pounded so loud I was sure you'd hear. I was just gonna leave and come back later to make sure you were all right."

Blinking and starting to shiver in the open doorway, she listened to him uncomprehendingly, watching the quizzical smile on his face while he talked.

"Hey." He came toward her, moved her into the house in front of him and shut the door. "Shouldn't be in a draft with bare feet."

Standing in the porch together then, she saw his nostrils flare slightly to the warm, sluggish scent of her, remembered the sleep clinging to her hair and face, and was embarrassed, suddenly excruciatingly embarrassed at his eyes on her loose breasts under the shirt, her bare, vulnerable feet. And then she was awake, angry, rubbing hard at her eyes with her knuckles.

"What do you want?" She sensed the querulous tone in her voice but could not prevent that even for his pleasant face.

"Dad sent me over to clear your driveway with the bucket." He laughed gently. "Heh, it's not a crime to sleep in once in a while. Are you scared I'm gonna tell on you?"

He was grinning at her as if they had a conspiracy, and she could not suppress her own small, sour smile. "I'm always up by eight to feed the pigs. I don't understand why I didn't wake up."

"Yeah, I thought they looked a little bit hungry."

"You were in the barn?" Hands on her hips she confronted his casual trespassing of her private ground.

He held up his hands. "Hold on—I just stood in the door to see if you were there. I swear I didn't go any further. Those mad sows of yours wanted to tear me to pieces. You should have heard them!"

She turned away, uneasy at his intrusion. "They're not mad. They're just not used to strangers." Still ungracious, she said, "Well, do you want some coffee?"

"Sure, that'd be perfect." He stooped to remove his boots, fingers quick and easy on the laces, the small, neat hands of a salesman not a farm boy, nails oval and ivory as if he buffed them every day. Then followed her bare feet on his stockinged ones into the kitchen, pulling out a chair from the table as if it were his own instead of a strange chair in a kitchen he had never entered.

Spooning coffee into the basket of the pot, she was almost surprised to see him there, Mina's son, sitting easily and looking around. The son of the woman she had spent an entire afternoon with last week, an afternoon that chased itself to nothing so quickly, words bending and unfolding around each other in the dusty barn.

The chair tipped back, held by the muscles of his thighs tight under his denim jeans, he was so perfectly at ease, so autonomous. And so different from the faint threads of him she preserved from that supper at his house—no, at Mina's house. His mother, Mina. He was nothing but an extension of her, yet here he was alone and complete in Judith's kitchen, overtaking it, as relaxed as if it were his own and she was his too.

"How's your mother?" She set the pot on the electric burner with a bang and twisted the knob.

"Hmm? Oh Mom, same as always."

She tried to plumb his indifference to his mother, that indifference born of proximity and a casual acceptance of what he considered his due. "Mina's a wonderful person." And looking at him, knew at once she sounded facetious, insincere to him, so casual and relaxed, waiting for her to fix his coffee, to perk it for five minutes and pour it into the mug.

He shrugged, Mina and mother not the same to him. Uncaring, he let his eyes explore her kitchen, seeking her out in the corners of the room and the pictures on the walls. So that she felt herself tighten, knew that under his careless, easy manner he was probing into her.

"Why didn't you bring her with you?"

His mouth quirked. "I came on the tractor. She said to tell you she'll be over tomorrow or the day after. Why don't you ever come over to our place instead?" It was his mouth that moved, that expressed what his face did not, quick and subtle, the outlines of his lips showing what his words slipped over.

"I think she likes to get away from you guys sometimes," she said pointedly. "And I don't have much to get away from here."

He laughed. "I guess she does get tired of us. Bad enough having one man in the house, let alone four."

She turned and lifted the bubbling coffee pot off the burner. His placidity distressed her, so uninjured, she could not be sure whether he offended or pleased her. She poured coffee into two mugs and carried them to the table, her bare feet feeling the cool smoothness of the floor. Beyond the window the magpie hopped in the snow. Setting the cup down, her fingers on the handle of the thick ceramic mug, she was suddenly shaken with a swift awareness, the glaring white fact of herself in front of his sardonic grin, clear as an etching.

Faint lines of dirt cracked in the creases of her hand on the handle of the mug; her fingernails were jagged and torn. Though she scrubbed them hard with soap and nailbrush, she never trimmed them, left them to split and tear from day to day, not even examining them the way that women do, meditative and preoccupied. Through the heat from the cup she felt the callouses on her palms, small hard pads, and his eyes on the back of her hand red and chapped from the cold. She snatched her hand away, angry at his casual intake of every part of her, ran her hand over her face, then caught herself and forced that hand to the table to pick up the cup, to ignore the questions in his eyes.

She saw herself as he must, slovenly and vulnerable, a woman with no care for herself, and wanted desperately to change that, to show him Judith instead, her hands soft and white, nails long and painted. Different then, her hands danced over the typewriter keys, held the razor-thin sheets of paper that slid into the roller of her typewriter. Paper cuts every day, invisible slices, the smallest cut the deepest; she sucked at them, squeezed her hands between her thighs to ease them and comfort them. And found them smudged with ink from the typewriter ribbon, the copy machine—beautiful hands but helpless, weak and injured. She longed then to strengthen them, to peel potatoes and carrots, to grind dirt into their creases; but cherished them instead, standing over the bathroom sink to wash away the ink after changing the typewriter ribbon. The sign on the wall: "Please keep this bathroom clean as other people use it too." Guiltily she rinsed ink off the bar of white soap and threw the crumpled paper towel in the garbage can. Washed her hands at least once an hour, standing in front of the gleaming sink under the glaring florescent lights in the antiseptic smell of room deodorizer.

Funny, there was never more than one woman in the bathroom at a time, never any talk in front of the mirrors or between the cubicles: "Hey, is there any paper in yours?" Sometimes, perversely, she went into a cubicle and waited, but no one ever came in. There must be some rule she didn't know, one at a time, no socializing in the bathroom, no fraternizing with colleagues. She automatically turned off the light when she left the bathroom; but when she came back an hour later, ink on the ends of her fingers from the leaky company pens, the light was always on again. Washed her hands as she met her own eyes in the big mirror hour after hour, marking the days, water over her fingers.

She sat down across from him at the table, feeling less awkward with her bare feet hidden. She hated his intrusion even as she welcomed it, felt a deep-seated response to the interest in his eyes, his invisible intention.

"Well?" But for the curiosity in his smile, they could have been married, an average morning pair.

"Well what?" Without really intending to, she still sounded grumpy, a child wakened before she is rested.

"So I find you're really our neighbor. You were a little hard to believe the other night."

"Why?" She said it quickly, defensive against that reiteration of her strangeness, her infidelity to expectations.

"We thought you'd be a stringy old maid of about thirty-five. Dad didn't tell us you were young and pretty."

"I'm not."

"Well, you're not stringy and sour anyway. I guess for Dad most women look the same."

"I doubt it," she said dryly.

He laughed. "How do I know?" And bent his head to the coffee cup to sip quietly, self-conscious.

Sitting across from him, she was as far

away as she could get but still too familiar, the placing one of intimacy. Just so her mother and father, the mornings emphasizing their quick, vibrant connection while she sat between them, connected and separate at the same time: her mother tousled and absentminded over toast and coffee, her father's head bent as he ate porridge, absorbed, eating quickly and mechanically, as farmers do, never enough time for leisure.

She watched him, the same duck of the head, yet so much more confident than the others, sure of himself. And Mina's son too. He was returning her stare openly, black lashes around dark-blue eyes flecked with gray above the stubborn ridge of his nose. She bent her head away from his gaze.

He finished his coffee quickly, some anxiety making him hurry. She suddenly wished him to stay and talk, not wanting to crunch the snow underfoot to the bottom of the hill, to open the door, to have to speak to the pigs. And he sensed it, oh yes, he sensed her small, unopened wish like the pursuer he was, and slowing himself to it instantly, put his elbows on the table and leaned toward her.

"Hey, Judy, do you just sit around here on weekends?"

She studied her nails, how quickly taken again that self-conscious motion of modesty that women assume under scrutiny. "I don't really notice the weekends."

"Don't you do anything?"

"Oh, I go shopping in town." Defensively, "I'm really busy with the pigs, you know."

He was awkward suddenly, knowing he shouldn't ask but asking anyway, his lips tense with the question. "Don't you have any family at all, Judy?" The name stemming from her bare feet, her ruffled hair.

"Oh yes," she said brightly, "there's my parents."

JAMES AUGUST PIERCE, 1903–1973.
AILEEN JANICE PIERCE, wife of the above, 1912–1973.

He looked at her, the quality of her reply carrying some tonal intimation he distrusted but could not touch, her face blank and shielded from him under a mask of determination.

"Brothers and sisters?"

"No, I was an only child. As a matter of fact, the late child of a very late marriage. My father was forrty-nine when I was born."

Leaving to mourn one daughter, Judith Pierce, of Edmonton.

Alone on the front bench of the funeral chapel, everything white and black mottled with shadow; the gray decency of the two coffins the only frivolity brass handles gleaming through the thick, subdued air. They could have been sitting together at breakfast, positioned so perfectly with her as a matrix, again the reference point in their grid. She sat forward, still hunched a little with the surprise and the outrage of it—oh, not the sudden swoop of fate that had robbed them of their leisure in their old age but her own abandonment, alone on a highly polished imitation pew listening to carefully sculpted organ notes unconnected to the actuality before her, their togetherness always, even apart. But it had been she who welded it and kept it and polished it, and now they had split that infinitesimal connection and she was alone, Judith.

"Funny," he said. "You don't seem like an only child. They're usually so spoiled."

She shook her head, silently backing away

from her aloneness. And he followed her again, so clean and effortless. Maybe it was the one moment he could catch at; maybe he had been waiting for it.

"Well, if you're not busy Friday night, why don't you let me teach you how to curl?"

"No." She shook her head too quickly.

He leaned toward her. "Why not? Come on, Judy, you can't spend all your time cooped up here."

"One of my sows will probably be coming in." No, not excuses, she needed to refuse. She was suddenly afraid of him, his insistence, his interest.

"Well, look, you can worry about that then. If a sow's coming in, we can make it Saturday. But you're gonna come, okay?"

"I can't just run off and leave them."

He was standing now, looking down at the still-sleepy blur of her oval face. "Look, you've gotta get out and do something. You'll go crazy if you just stay here, Judy."

"Don't call me Judy!" She flung the words at him, wanting to hurt him.

"Sorry." The single word was stiff and tight on his lips and he turned toward the door. "I'll plow out the drive. The snow's stopped now."

Bending to lace his boots, the back of his neck vulnerable between the edge of his dark hair and his coat collar, she wanted suddenly to touch him and had to stop herself, shrinking before his magnetism.

"Thanks for waking me up. I might have slept all day."

His eyes slid over her face, searching for the tongue of her inflection, her lack of commitment. "I doubt it." Hand curving around the doorknob, he turned back to her with an unexpected grin. "I'll drop around Friday. Maybe you'll change your mind." He winked. "And I promise I won't tell anybody that I caught you in bed."

He was out the door, legs black as spiders against the pristine snow; then hauling himself onto the looming tractor, ruptured it into a roar. Perched above the threat of its jerking power he maneuvered it against the snow, the shovel blades creasing a scar into the banks along the drive.

She watched from the window until he was gone, then went to find her socks.

Eight

In the coldness of the morning she struggled, wrestled herself into jeans and thick socks and flannel shirt, a repetition of so many days before. She dodged through the living room, formal teakwood and rough tweed upholstery tinged with leftover urban formality, uninviting to the splintery brittleness of her emerging bones and muscles.

In the bathroom she splashed cold water on her face and toweled it roughly, rubbing the cloth over her hair as well; and without stopping to face herself in the mirror, dragged on an overcoat and boots and forced herself out the door, the finality of its closing opening her day. In the instant and chill penetration of the air there was direction, pushing her down the hill so that her touch then grasp on the icy iron handle of the barn door was almost eager.

Her feet on the worn edges, following the stairs into the still-dim kitchen that waited for her mother, she would let herself into the gray air, stumbling and still half blind with sleep, to the red mass of the barn. She fumbled open the door to let her body plunge into the hot pungency of the barn, farrowing sows and steaming yellow piss and electric rat-like piglets pink under the light. And her father in his crooked attitude of weighted labor, shaking chop out of a five-gallon pail over the board fence. Standing beside him, she reached out to touch the rough brown wool of his coat, and he turned to her, setting down the pail to lay a blunt and heavy hand on her shoulder, so that they stood together almost lovers in the pale light of morning.

Ears perked and forward, the pigs scrambled to their feet when Judith turned on the light and spoke the day's beginning. They moved to the front of the pen to whoof and grunt as she walked between them, the force and matrix of the barn. And even with her hands still huddled in her pockets and shivering with revulsion for their wrinkled snouts and bristling hides, she must have loved them passionately for giving her a reason to be alone in the morning—to utter her first words to them.

Rolling away from his stirring limbs, the weight of his arm across her back demanding, she hid her face in the fabric of the pillow to edge out his wakened and eager voice. Could tolerate him shaven and cool and clothed, even with that unquenchable analysis in his eyes, all-knowing and appraising of her clothed or naked, it mattered little which. But like this—his limbs heavy and concentrated beside hers, the weight of his bones a slope for her to roll against, the rub of his hair against her chafed and muted skin—he was unbearable.

"Judith?"

"Mmm?"

"Are you awake?"

"No."

Silence. "Then why are you talking to me?"

"I'm not."

But already his arms around her, pinning her from behind and shaping his body to hers, knees drawn up and fetal, surrounding her like a shell.

"You ugly critters."

Snuffing the scent of her into their nostrils,

they enveloped her in the concentrated aura of their milk, their piss, their shit, the sweat of their hides, the earth of their cloven hooves. Like so many devils, she thought, red eyes and all, peering at her through the dust-filtered haze of the barn.

She laid a hand on the yellow boards. Marie Antoinette thrust a massive head over the fence beside it, her breath blowing moistly. "I'm sorry, Marie Antoinette, but I feel itchy today."

She hesitated there, chewing her lips as she rubbed that hand over the board fence. "You're not . . ." And she could have been talking to herself, the shapings of her tongue and lips unsubstantial and incomplete. "Hell." She swung away, bulky in the winter coat, stamped up and down the aisle until she stopped again, hesitated, then almost blurted the words, her voice low and furious. "Hell, I need a man. A good, honest fuck."

And this time her hand sought the fence blindly, grasped its rough edge in an unseeing need for support, leaned against it, head drooping. White-knuckled, that red and roughened hand gripped the board beside the fleshy jowls that hung below Marie Antoinette's pursed and wrinkled snout.

Heads uptilted and unblinking, they regarded her from their lower height, the piglets snuffing the woman smell about her and eyeing the inclination of her too-rigid body. Curious, her aloneness. They had expected another like her or like the man who had stood so briefly in the doorway that morning when they waited so long for her to come. Appearing suddenly, the man had startled them into movement, their mother scrambling her forelegs onto the fence to raise herself, body shaking with the violence of her whoofs and grunts, red madness in her eyes as she gnashed her long teeth in his direction. And they caught only a glimpse of his suppleness, the twist at the corners of his mouth, a derisive indentation in his cheek.

Quiet now, they waited for her movement, only an occasional snuffle or scrabble in the straw betraying them. She lifted her head and allowed a faint laugh at their expectant faces. Clapped her hands, "Shoo!" so that they scrambled around the circumference of the pen.

She reached out that too-still hand again to scratch the creases behind Marie Antoinette's ear, talking softly now. "When you don't want them you'll do anything to get rid of them, and when you've gotten rid of them you want them back." How do you stop once you've started? she thought. Oh, how do you stop once you've started? How do you get rid of it without upsetting all those tricky balances you've lined up into rows and made bargains with yourself about.

Bargains. Hell, Judith. She had to stop for a moment at five, stop and hesitate, clinging to the handrail and looking up the tunnel of the gray cement stairwell. Come on, only three more flights. Where's your guts? You're getting fat and out of shape, can't do anything anymore. Except screw. And she climbed furiously again, her body fluttering with weakness. On the eighth floor she went into the washroom, combed her hair and mopped the beads of sweat from her forehead with a paper towel.

Eight flights four times a day should be equal to two miles. Five times a week, ten miles. Her body slumped at the idea and she pulled herself erect, turned sideways to look at its profile in the mirror. She clenched her teeth, looking at her midriff, the slight bulge appearing at her waist. Turning into a blob, her ass on the typewriter chair, her legs crossed under the desk, her hands white and well-cared-for, body pale and grub-like under his. Sliding behind her desk she watched Clara's heavy shape bending over a filing cabinet. Her breasts overflowed their confinement, her thick legs were planted squarely apart. I wonder, she thought, I wonder if he ever . . . No. She covered her eyes with her hand, then pushed herself back from the desk.

"Clara, I'm going out for a minute. I have to go to the bank."

"Sure." Clara did not turn from the open file. "But the bank doesn't open until ten. It's barely nine o'clock."

"Well, I have to mail a letter before the first pickup."

"Okay by me. I'll watch your phone." Clara slammed the drawer and placidly shoved herself behind her typewriter while Judith flailed into her coat.

"I'll be right back."

"Sure."

Outside she walked the mid-morning deserted streets frantically, hands deep in her pockets and her breath leaving puffs of vapor in the December air. Stragglers on the now gray and colorless sidewalks were a mild reminder of the bustling afternoon crowds.

She bit her lip. Oh no, anything but that—fat and complacent, predictable. Already the lethargy was settling on her bones, heavy and unwieldy. Through the cold stinging her face, she thought of Judy floating down the steep stairs, her feet strong and sure, movement so practiced it was almost like flying. She hung in swift grace, suspended above the stairway, before hauling on the old red coat and flying to the barn.

So that Judith thought they were a part of her, the children bursting around the corner, coats and scarves flapping around the fluidity of their bones, voices disembodied in the icy air. They parted just before her legs, then joined again to leave her in the swirl of their motion. She stood for a long moment looking after them, then turned her steps back to the office, the stale mustiness of heated air enveloping her while she waited for the elevator. She rode it to the eighth floor, numbly loosening her coat.

Beyond the partition the sound of her shovel and pails aroused the pigs—hungry and expectant they awaited the ritual: chop and water and straw. Under the reassurance of their unchanging demands, her rigidity eased; the security of sameness, birth and suckling, eating and excreting, sleeping and waking, their golden eyes always watching. And it could even have been shame that made her subside, a fear of her own too-quick plunges and backtrackings.

Humorless she was, with that piled-up heap of expectations and that determination to recreate her lost chance even while she hated it and them, chop and shit and the ache in her back. And she was even more afraid of that, her own craziness creeping out from inside, talking to herself in that empty house while she worked on her penny-by-penny books and planned what she would do when they were big enough to be weaned and she would have to buy a boar.

She hated the idea, a boar; another chunk out of the money at the bank and still no return, not to mention another pen to build, with a big enough space for him to breed the sows. She brooded over it, lavished them with chop and water and clean straw, and supervised another birthing, calling the sow Daisy this time, after Daisy Buchanan, because she was reading the book at the time.

That was the one thing she did, borrowed the books that Mina borrowed from the lending library in town. She avoided going herself, only drove into the larger town twice a month for groceries and necessities.

But she went into Norberg every second day, the truck making its four-mile journey like clockwork; and once there, not the store or the café, but entering the post office, standing quietly in the eleven o'clock clot of waiting farmers and villagers, hands in her pockets and head down while they stared at her and talked around her. Until the postmaster banged the wicket open and the slow talk stopped, some of them surging to the numbered metal boxes to click them open and reach for the contents with stubby fingers, others lining up to ask the white-haired man presiding over General Delivery the inevitable, "Any mail today?"

She lined up with them, denied her own autism in that patient wait for a few circulars and form letters. Never a private, handwritten envelope that she could call personal. Maybe she expected it, that he would discover her and write to ask her for some explanation. If she did she must have been disappointed, all those mornings in the post office waiting for something to come, the letters of her name on a white square reaffirming whatever it was she wanted.

And whatever held her in that myopic stasis? Fear of the possibility of her insanity, the sheer magnitude of her quiet but frantic scrabbling to regain what she thought she had lost? Always there was the image in her mind of the gaunt, gray woman who came walking across the pasture one day, wearing rubber boots and an elaborate church social hat, the hem of her dress muddy to her knees. It was her voice, the different accent on the vowels, that Judy remembered most. Her mother made the woman come in and have some tea, but she stayed only a short time before she drifted off across the pasture again, as vacant and aimless as she had come. Her mother shook her head after her, murmuring, "Poor woman," while Judy persisted, "What's the matter with her? Why does she talk so funny?"

"She comes from England," said her mother absently, "and a dairy farm in central Alberta . . ." still shaking her head. Judy knew that England was across the sea. But the inflection of her mother's pity made her wonder: was everyone from England sad like that?

It was her father who answered the real question. "She doesn't have enough to do, brooding all the time. Ought to get her mind on work and she'd be fine." And she had believed him, oh yes, her all-knowing father with a cure for everything.

That could have been what she was trying to remember, Judith, that afternoon when the furtive idea brushed through her mind. Her fingers slipped over the keyboard with a rhythm of their own, an intricate patterned dance following the pattern of her eyes on the pattern of the words, eyes never leaving the guiding page beside her while her fingers leapt and sang to the small hum of the stolid machine. She played it, moving into an almost-awareness with the ends of her incredibly swift fingers, not one letter missed, the words forming on the white page as if divined; from the guide to her eyes to her fingers to the page in the sheer instant of perfection she could almost attain by keeping this up she would have it, the perfect page inscribed with the implacable truth she was looking for.

"Judith, could you see that this gets done before 4:30?"

She stared up at him for a moment, uncomprehending, then instantly perceived his arrogance, so casual and confident and unaware of her privateness, felt her face whiten and a sickening flood of black, pitted rage against him.

suddenly saw the clear outlines of the vague, sluggish thought she had been half-heartedly pursuing in her helplessness against him, and knew just as suddenly what she had to do. First the child in the racing cluster of children that morning and now this intrusion, and she was suddenly perfectly sure.

So that she decided in the winter and it took until the next winter to even get close to vindicating it, and until the fall after that winter to leave, and now it was winter again and here she was regretting it. Oh, not that much. But she wanted more. It was evident in the way she shouldered feed and water pails with the listless energy born of necessity, confided in the pigs that she wanted a man.

It all pivoted back to her father, guilt and desire; thick and bent as he was, it was really him she wanted. In the feed mill, "This is my girl, Judy." Not the little girl, but the half-grown girl, gracefully awkward with that unstudied lack of awareness that she carried like a knapsack, that she hung on to as carefully as she failed to know it.

They were never satisfied. "Hey, Jim, she oughta be a boy. Whatdya say, Judy, wouldn't it be better if you were a boy?" Swinging their heels and drinking coffee in the UFA office shack.

From behind that curtain of reserve she gazed at them with an infallible and unblinking stolidness, refusing even to speak.

"Nah." Her father's hand on her shoulder pressed reassurance. "Judy's better'n a boy. Not so clumsy."

"Hah." They laughed together, heedless of her crouched and wincing face. "You're gettin' soft, Jim."

Finally the grain would be ground and the feed loaded. In the truck she sat against the door as far away from him as possible until he turned his head and looked at her. "Don't listen to 'em," he said. "Don't bother listenin' to 'em."

And then they smiled at each other, father and daughter, their perfect joining. That was what she fell back on now, mumbling to the pigs under her breath and sweat matting her hair. That was the last-minute resource that she held just under the surface; it was her father that stood in black relief against the winter, against her desire.

Nine

And then at night the pigs heard the sound, seeping through the barn walls, through the warmth and luminosity of the sheltering wood, the call drifted over their instantly attentive breathing. They could feel their mother, the firm skin of her belly that lay beside their snouts, stiffen and tense to the rise of that desolate and drawn-out wail, that eerie invitation to be still and listen. As one they hesitated, the concerted slumber in their drowsy and pungent envelope ruptured by the uncanny refrain. Stirring then, they rose and shuffled uneasily about their straw nests. The coyotes were far away, so distant and remote, but the sound was close and threatening.

In the house she heard them too, lying on her back with her hands locked behind her head. Against the rising inflection of their urgent keening she rose and crossed to the window. She held the curtain aside with one hand, hugging her naked body with the other, and looked out at the black, upward-pointing fingers of the poplars.

The grieving cry came again and she calculated that they were to the west, closer to the barn and the other side of the house. Involuntarily, she shivered. Winter creatures, creatures who slid across the snow like spirits, driven back only slightly by the encroachment of man, mocking in their tenacity, their hold on the small clumps of brush and the open fields. Coyotes.

She crawled back into bed and switched on the lamp on the bedside table. It was that they sounded so forsaken; the way they made everything seem desolate and forlorn. Drawing her knees up under the covers she hugged them, rocking her body back and forth.

Rocking herself while her mother sat on the chair beside the bed reading aloud in the rosy light from the pink-shaded lamp. Charles Dickens, those impossible tales that she listened to chapter by chapter, wide-eyed. Her mother's voice rising and falling in monotonous comfort until her father came in, rough and brisk with cold, to lean down to her and rub the icy redness of his face against hers so that she squealed and giggled. And turning away to go, still in his overcoat. "Sow gonna come in tonight."

Beside him her mother was still and dull. Suddenly she shuddered. "Listen, James . . ."

The sound penetrated the room from far; it floated dreamy and irresistible. Judy felt icy fingers run along her spine.

"Coyotes," he said, head high and entranced. "Coyotes."

"Ugh, I hate them." Her mother's hand was at her throat, white and frightened.

"Why do they cry like that?" Judy asked soberly, her pity coming before her fear.

He laughed. "Because they're varmints and they want you to feel sorry for them. They'll sing you to sleep."

Stretching her body along the narrow bed, Judith sighed and reached to switch off the light. Coyotes. Another pleading cry rose and fell. She rolled over onto her stomach and slept.

But tramping down the path to the barn the next morning she caught a stealthy movement out of the corner of her eye and turned to see him trotting away, head high and tongue lolling, his tail sweeping the snow.

"Scram, you sneak," she yelled. "I've got nothing for you to steal."

He ignored her and ambled off, as self-possessed as if she had never spoken.

In the barn she was immediately surrounded by the pigs, the warmth and sibilance of their procreation, the whispered shuffle of their rising. She inspected them, walking the length of the barn and back so scrupulously, her eyes following every detail of their snuffling movement. Enacting the ritual—hanging her coat, gathering pails, feed, water, clean straw—they could see it was becoming her systematic and deliberate liturgy, an ordering of her time and body. She was as contingent on them as they were on her.

And this day, for the first time, in the quiet exposure of the winter light, she cut the strings on the boxes packed so hurriedly four months ago in her city apartment. She remembered sitting in the middle of the floor in a nest of her possessions, the refuse of those years, thrusting into boxes the photographs and scrapbooks and ticket stubs and backless evening dresses that she wished to hurl into the garbage bin but could not, would cart with her like deadwood. Chinese spoons and candlesticks and scented stationery, she packed with the finality of desperation, already stifling the urge to turn back then.

Lifting those fragments out of their newspaper packing, she was surprised to find them so light, so lifeless in her hands, and she wondered why she had waited so long, why she had viewed the boxes with apprehension when they had so little significance, contained only dusty objects that aroused neither pain nor regret.

And so she could put them away in this,

her new house, carelessly, untroubled by their past; could even think of using them like a gift given by someone she hardly knew, with no implications or reminders. And if he were to appear there on her doorstep, would she handle him the same way? Even in her denial, she might have wished for him to come, to persuade her to abandon everything for him again.

When the short light began to fade, she went to the barn, leaving half-opened boxes and their contents to clutter her living room. This time she closed the barn door thoughtfully and was only jolted out of her reverie when she found another sow down and farrowing.

"I should have known," she said, and they heard her running foosteps crunching the snow to the house. She was back immediately, the heat lamp clutched in her mittened hand, her absentmindedness completely gone in the face of another birthing. A good thing too, this one so painful and laborious, the sow grinding her teeth with savage misery and her racking breath creating a wake of stillness in the pigs. The piglets were backwards, blue and gasping by the time they arrived, one of them dead, black inside the gray mass of his sack.

Crouching in the straw beside the sow, her voice rose and fell, the words smoothing the sow's ragged groans, almost a song: "It's all right, come on now, push, don't stop . . ." And after the second dead one, waxy and as still as marble, she knew what she had to do and she rolled up her right sleeve. Drawing a deep breath she reached her hand and then her arm into that interminable, hot liquid tunnel that closed on her like a vise, and inside there she groped through the folds until she touched the futile hindquarters of a piglet. She grabbed him, feeling his body under her fingers, and pulled him out. He lay limp and boneless. She rubbed him vigorously with straw until he began to gasp small, angry inhalations.

And again she reached her hand into that seething passage and again her hand closed on a feeble body and again she guided him down that endless avenue to light and air. Again and again until, staggering through the straw, there were eight living piglets that she had induced to life, and only two born dead.

And then her hand could find nothing more. Standing, small electric needles darted through her legs and she had to clutch the fence with her left hand, her bared right arm bloody to the elbow, blood staining the rolled-up sleeve of her flannel shirt.

Under the icy water from the chorehouse tap she washed it off, water so cold it numbed her skin just as the sow's scorching tunnel had seemed to burn it.

Back inside the pen she sat weak and drained on a chunk of straw bale, watching the staggering piglets and the now-quiet sow. Musing there, with her head on her arms, she realized that it was Friday, the weekend. It was all the same here, one day merged into the next. She thought of those weekends, Judith covering her typewriter with a quiet elation, going home to lie full-length in the tub, brushing and brushing her hair, painting her nails, until his key clicked in the lock. Sitting behind heavy-covered menus and across white-clothed tables, dancing quietly around hardwood floors, to come back to the apartment and prepare for bed, not falling on each other now but sitting on the edge of the bed to pull off their shoes, taking time to undo buttons and hang clothes in the closet. They might have been married, their habits so predictable and customary. There was no longer even any need for conversation. And for a while then she would feel safe, lying beside him in her darkened bedroom.

Suddenly Marie Antoinette whoofed and Judith jerked her head up. The barn door opened and slammed and Jim came around the corner of the chorehouse, face shining and hands in his pockets.

"Hey, why are you sitting out here?" he demanded. "I thought you'd be ready."

As one, the sows rose and growled, grunting and snorting at his voice. The piglets scurried back and forth in the pen, squealing and snorting.

She looked at him blankly, blinking at his cheerful disparagement, then suddenly came alive. "Hey, be quiet! You're disturbing my pigs."

He pulled a face. "Pardon me."

"Just shut up and stand still."

She climbed over the fence and went up and down the pens, clicking her tongue, talking quietly until the sows emitted only an occasional grunt and stood watching the man, their red eyes wary and unblinking. Only the piglets raced back and forth through the straw, coming to a dead halt, then skittering off around the pen again.

There was a stranger in the barn. He smelled as sharp and rank as grass, the emanation from his skin dark and wanton. A strange excitement made them scamper madly through the straw, a pure sensation in the air that was a mixture of them, the woman and the man.

He stood beside the pen with the new piglets. The furious sow struggled to get her feet beneath her, whoofing with rage. Judith slid over the fence like water, knelt beside her and laid her hand on the sow's flank. "Whoa, Emily, take it easy there. Lie still. You'll hurt yourself."

Until the sow stopped thrashing and lay panting angrily.

"Do you give them names?" he asked curiously.

She looked up at him. "Hey, what exactly do you want this time? I don't like strangers in here. It upsets everybody."

"Pigs are more important than me? I came to take you curling." His voice was candid and innocent.

She stood up and heaved an exasperated sigh, hands on her hips. "I told you, *No!*"

He shrugged and grinned at her disarmingly. "I thought you might have changed your mind."

"I haven't. Besides, my sow just finished having piglets."

"She's done—great! That means you'll come."

"No way. I haven't fed or watered the others yet and I have to break the teeth out. And anyway, I'm not ready to go anywhere."

"If I help you, you'll be done in ten minutes."

"You can't help me."

"Why not? I know how to feed pigs."

"Not my pigs. It has to be done a certain way and I've got to do it myself."

"Well, I'll just sit on a bale then and watch you. I don't mind watching a woman work."

"It's pointless for you to wait. I'm not going anywhere."

"What are you worried about? I'm not going to attack you."

Confronted then with his directness, she could only evade him. "It's just that I don't care about curling. I hate sports. I'm a spectator."

"Well, then we'll go and spectate. Better yet, we'll go to the bar and have a couple of draft. Haven't done that with a girl for a long time."

"Why not?"

"Too young," he said briefly, and she remembered Mina telling her that he liked high school girls.

"Well, why don't you pick on them?"

"Boring." His voice was suddenly gentle, persuasive. "Come on, Judy, it's a lovely night. Too bad to waste it."

She said nothing, and avoiding his eyes picked up her pails and clanked to the chorehouse with them. Around the corner of the partition she called "Do you want to fill these pails with water while I break the babies' teeth out?" Then eyed the crease in his clean blue jeans. "No, wait, you'll get yourself all dirty."

"Filling a couple of pails from a tap is not going to make me dirty." He took the pails from her hands.

She lifted the tooth clipper from the hook and went to Emily's pen. Grasping the wriggling piglets firmly behind their ears, she snapped the tiny fangs with brutal speed. She set the last piglet down gently beside the sow, to find him standing by the pen, watching her. "You handle that little cutter pretty well."

"I have to," she said pointedly, brushing the white shards off the blades with a small handful of straw. She threw her legs over the fence and walked to the chorehouse to hang up the clipper.

"Who taught you?" he asked, following behind her.

"My father." Unnecessarily, "He taught me everything." And could have bitten her tongue off after she said it.

He threw back his head and laughed aloud, the unfamiliar sound of it again rousing the pigs to frantic whoofs and grunts.

"Look," she said, "do you mind? My pigs are not used to your kind of noise."

"Don't you ever laugh?"

"Not at nothing."

"Sorry." Still smiling at her, still watching her face.

Tranquil and easy, he waited, ready to wait for a day. She measured the feed with extra care, weighed it out as if it were a precious metal. Plodded through the feeding so slowly, so methodically, that the front pigs had almost eaten their chop by the time she brought their water. He wanted to lift the water pails for her but she refused, made him set them down in the aisle.

"I've got to do it myself. Every pig needs a certain amount, and every pig is different."

So that he stood out of her way and whistled, hands in his pockets, while she swung the pails and poured the water carefully, so carefully, and banged the pails down again. Until finally there was nothing left to do and she walked up and down the row of pens trying to remember some leftover chore but could not and he was standing there watching her sardonically and she had to say ungraciously, "Okay, I guess that's it."

In the kitchen he sat at the table and looked through her stack of hog journals while she showered. When he heard the water spray stop, his lips twitched in the ghost of a grin and he shouted to her, "Don't dress up. It'll seem less like a date then."

A moment later she came into the kitchen dressed in clean denim and a dark sweater, the ends of her damp, ragged hair already drying. "I wasn't going to. Jeans is all you get."

"Good enough for me."

"Forget the compliments. We can go in five minutes when my hair is dry."

"Sure." He flipped the magazine shut. "After all this, I'm just surprised you're really coming with me."

"Maybe I've decided you're harmless. And, after all, it was you who reminded me what a nice night it is."

"A great night to go looking for fun."

"No fun." She said it quickly and firmly, even afraid to joke about it.

"Okay." And again there was the irrepressible grin, that quick twist of his lips at her nervousness.

"Hey," she said suddenly, "I haven't had any supper. I better have a sandwich. Do you want one?"

"Sure." He watched her, grinning while she banged cupboard doors and buttered bread.

Sitting at either end of the table, a repetition of the first morning he came, they ate, silent and absorbed. And then both raised their heads, listened as the thin, high knife of sound sliced into the night.

"There they go again," she said. "I heard them yesterday."

"Spooky. Are you afraid of them?"

She shook her head briefly. "My mother was. She said the sound always made her believe something terrible was going to happen."

She hesitated then, remembering she had told him that her parents were alive; then thought that he must have recognized the lie by now. He said nothing but sat with his head on one side, listening to the plummet of the prolonged, icy cry.

She picked up her plate and put it in the sink. "Let's go."

And he stood too, instantly attentive. "I'm ready when you are."

In the truck on the way to Norberg they said little. She sat close to the door on her side, careful not to extend any invitation. When they entered town he looked at his watch. "Too late to go to the curling rink," he said. "Let's try the bar." He pulled up in front of the hotel, the entire ground floor alight under a painted sign that creaked in the wind, carrying a ridge of snow: Licensed premises.

They entered into a hot, sour smell of sweaty bodies and spilled beer. Unlike city bars, the place was brightly lit. Judith blinked, the dimness of all those lounges after work, sipping martinis as they huddled together over a table, his hand stroking her leg, and that dullness in her head after the third one so that his face wavered and became featureless and blank. Once she called him Norman, her voice maneuvering heavily around the words. Instantly his face revived, the features sharp and clear, eyes like solid lead. He leaned toward her, his mouth so close and speaking so quietly that she saw the words rather than heard them. "You little bitch." And she felt only an overwhelming bewilderment, not anger or pain but a blurred surprise at his restrained ferocity. Maybe that was where her resentment began, his fierce control in the face of her confusion.

In keeping with its imitation of a lounge, the hotel bar boasted a dark-brown carpet, spotted with cigarette burns and indefinable stains, the round tables covered with orange toweling from which the acrid smell of beer seemed to emanate more strongly than anywhere else.

She thought of that time in the Stettler bar with Norman, her father never in the bar—"Too busy working to sit around all day and gab." She had never been in a bar before, Judy twisting her fingers together in her lap while the ALCB glass of amber liquid stood untouched in front of her.

At the table beside them, some truckers or

cowboys stared and poked each other in the ribs, talking loud enough for her to hear.

"I wonder what that ugly, skinny guy is doin' with that sweet-lookin' girl?" Exploding into guffaws, heavy and handsome and at ease, while she sat taut and anxious. "Maybe we should knock him out and steal her!"

So terrified she was that when they were finally in the car she cried, holding her hands in front of her face to hide it from him.

Driving, he glanced at her, his mouth stubborn and thin. "What in hell's the matter with you, Judy?"

So that she cried harder, and for one mad instant felt herself reaching for the door handle to fling herself out of the car, away from his blunt stupidity.

"You're awfully quiet," Jim said.

"Just thinking. It's been a long time since I was in a country bar."

He held up four fingers and the waiter, who was also bartender, brought four glasses.

She picked up a glass and drank, the same bitter, unyielding taste.

"These places are pretty unexciting." He looked around and waved at a clot of men sitting a couple of tables away. "Just farmers mostly. No crazies like you see in the city bars."

She looked at him. "There's crazies everywhere."

He raised his eyebrows, waited.

"You are," she said, smiling, that small and awkward joke as tentative as her own caution, but enough to make him laugh happily, enough to forge a brown warmth between them.

"Thanks, Judy. I'd be the last to deny it."

"For instance," she pursued, " you must be crazy to keep on calling me Judy when you know how much I hate it."

"You don't hate being called Judy," he

said, not looking at her but at the far end of the bar.

She hesitated. "I don't like it." Lamely, "It makes me feel like a kid."

"That's not why either," he said musingly. "Is it?"

She felt a sweep of anger then pushed it back, thinking, No, not now, don't spoil it. And was saved from having to answer by a gruff voice that rose out of a barrel chest standing beside their table.

"Jim. How ya doin? Been a long time since we saw ya in here. Quit robbin' the cradle, have ya?"

"Sure thing, Johnny. Gonna join us?"

He swayed a little. "Well, I wouldn't wanna innerupt. Just wanted to find out if this is the li'l lady who's raisin' pigs out there on Johnson's eighty over by the correction line."

He did not look at her but at the ceiling and she was tempted to answer him rudely. She glanced at Jim and he winked, a quick warning, so she said mildly, "Yes, I am."

"Well, that's innerestin'. Everybody around here's grain or cattle farmers. What you wanna raise pigs for?"

She could not help it, could not stop herself in the face of his bleary belligerence. "For fun," she said sharply.

He raised his hands. "Sorry, sorry, don't mean to bother you if you don't like my askin'."

"That's fine," she said tightly.

"Hey, Johnny . . ." Jim lowered his voice to a conspiratorial tone. "Lemme buy you a beer some other day. This is a heavy date."

He snorted. "Well, won't bother ya anymore. Nice t'ave met ya." He flapped a meaty red hand at them and lumbered back to his crowded table.

"Don't scowl at me. I didn't mean it," Jim

said to her. "It's the fastest way to get rid of him."

She nodded and turned her glass between her hands, watching the bubbles rise to the top.

"We were talking about your name," he said.

"Let's not."

"I can't help calling you Judy. It just slips out."

"You don't try," she said.

"Sure I do."

She made a face at him. "I think your mother's right. You're just used to hanging around kids."

The voices at the crowded table rose, and the farmers and young people scattered around the bar looked toward them curiously. One voice climbed above the others. "I wondered what that smell was—pig shit!" The table exploded into laughter.

She twisted in her chair and glared at them, ready to bite back, but Jim touched her arm urgently. "Take it easy, Judy. They're only kidding around."

She subsided unwillingly. "Oh, all right. Just as long as they don't keep it up."

The atmosphere seemed thicker and louder now, the quiet swallowed by raised voices and the thump of the jukebox. The bar that had appeared relaxed and half-empty when they arrived felt crowded and antagonistic. She sensed eyes on the back of her head, the gritty knowledge that they were talking about her.

"If they say anything else, just ignore it." Jim leaned toward her over the table. "They'll quit soon enough."

"Sure," she said sarcastically.

"Do you want to go?"

"No, I'm not leaving because of them."

Jim waved his hand at the waiter again.

There was a slight scuffle at the rowdy table, the whipping ends of an argument. Then a burly, red-haired man stood, swaying a little, a glass of beer held high above his head. "I'm gonna sing a song," he shouted, "for Jim's new lady." Suddenly the whole tavern was perfectly still, suspended motionless and hushed. The man cleared his throat, put his left hand on his chest, then began a chanting singsong in a deep, hoarse voice:

"Ahhhh, pigs can swim, pigs can fly,
Pigs they watch the wind go by,
Pigs make great household pets . . ."

His sandpaper voice was drowned in a wild rupture of laughter, and a moil of confusion thrust him into his chair with a bump, spilling his beer.

The waiter shouted to them from behind the bar, "You guys are gonna get kicked out if you don't . . ."

Inexplicably she was standing and the men turned to her, ignoring the waiter. Fierce and narrow-eyed she faced them. "What do you know about it? You guys drink too much and work too little."

"Judy . . ." Jim grabbed her arm. "It's only a joke."

"It's not funny," she gritted over her shoulder at him.

"Ah ha!" said Johnny. "Little lady's got spirit, I see. That's the way to pick 'em."

"Never know it to see 'er every day in that post office, waitin' for something to come," someone else chimed in.

She bared her teeth at them, hands clenched by her sides. "Who the fuck ever told you I was a lady?"

Jim was standing beside her. "Judy . . ."

But they only laughed, the whole table, how many were there, five or six exploding into a parody of mirth—coarse, abrasive guffaws that echoed and rebounded in the tavern. She was on her feet and facing them, that pack howling like coyotes in their field, brave because they were not alone, one supporting the other. And she thought irrelevantly that the lonely coyote call was the beautiful one, falling away against the crackling of the air to a faint, shivering moan that lingered beyond itself.

"Hey," one of them shouted. "She's cute when she's mad."

"Why don't you go piss up a rope?" she hissed.

"Judy . . ." Jim was frantically shaking her arm. "I don't want to get in a fight here."

She glanced at him and for a fleeting instant she saw the shadows behind his eyes, felt the warmth of his hand on her arm. Blindly she touched his hand with her doubled fist, gathering for a small instant some of his warmth there. Then she looked at the men again. "*I* do."

"Wait." Jim's voice was lost in their surge of protest.

"Hey, little lady, that's not a pretty thing to say."

"She really does get mad."

"C'mon," one of them said, "let's all have 'nother round and be fren'ly."

"Not with you." Her voice was low but it carried over the bar. "It's great to insult me but it's not nice to insult you, oh no. Well, you're an asshole."

The waiter rested a full tray of beer on the table and said to Jim, "If you can get them to listen, everybody gets a free beer on the house."

"What?" The singer scraped his chair back and detached himself from the group, menacing now.

Instinctively she reached for something, blindly raising a glass of the amber liquid from the waiter's tray. The burly man's sullen steps gave her no chance to hesitate or think, and she flung the frothy liquid full in his face.

He might have been a wounded bull, roaring in blind rage. He blundered into a table and upset it, the bar erupting around him in a pinwheel of flannel shirts and workboots. The waiter backed away, open-mouthed. Jim shouldered aside a man who flailed at Judith. Her small body ducked around him to fling another glass of foaming beer into the boiling men. They retreated, then rose and advanced, but now she was slinging beer, glass and all, her aim as hard and flexed as her set, furious face.

And then the owner was there, flinging bodies out of his way as she stood, still hurling frothy glasses from the full tray on the table beside her. And she did not even feel Jim's arm around her, only reached for another glass to feel her fingers close on air and realized that he was propelling her toward the door.

"Lemme go." She twisted against him as he dragged her down the two steps to the sidewalk. "Lemme go!"

"No way. Come on, you wanna get killed maybe?"

Jerking open the driver's side of the truck he shoved her in, then almost scrambled on top of her to get in himself, thrusting the key in the ignition and backing away just as the bouncer flung open the door and started down the steps after them. He drove madly, circling the town before heading out to the country and away from the direction of home.

"Where're you going?"

He did not answer but drove steadily, swinging around the curves and bumping over an unmarked railway track without looking.

Miles later, on a dark, quiet road, he pulled over to the side and stopped. Hands still on the wheel he stared straight ahead into a feather of snowflakes on the windshield.

"I want to go home," she demanded.

"Just give them a chance to cool down, will you?"

"Oh shit, surely they've had fights in that bar before."

He turned and looked at her steadily, then shook his head. "Sister, they are never gonna let you into that place again."

She shrugged. "So? Who cares?" She felt her hair. "Heck, I've got beer in my clean hair."

"And what about me? I enjoy my occasional draft."

"Sorry."

They were silent for a while, their breath steaming the cold windshield. "Well," he said finally, looking at her again, "I guess you sure got even with me."

She jerked up her head. "How?"

"I bug you to go out with me and so you start a fight in the Norberg bar."

"I didn't start it."

"You were the one who started throwin' beer."

"So what was I supposed to do? Be a lady? He needed to be taught a lesson." She slouched down on the seat and stared straight ahead. "You'd better take me home."

"Maybe you should stay at our place tonight."

"What for?"

"Well, if those guys get any bright ideas and come around bothering you . . ."

"Nah, they won't. They wouldn't have an audience. That was the whole idea."

"I don't know."

"No way. Besides, if they come, I can always phone you."

"Well, maybe you're right. I guess they've had their fun."

"Some fun."

He snorted. "You looked like you enjoyed slinging that beer at those guys."

She chuckled suddenly. "Maybe I did at that."

In the soft, pale light that was reflected into the truck cab from the snow-covered ground they looked at each other. Jim laughed quietly, the corners of his mouth twitching. "I'll never forget the look on Hiram's face when you threw that beer at him."

She giggled. "Is that his name? And he was making fun of my pigs?"

She bounced up on the seat and laughed outright, the crescendo of her glee rising and growing inside her until she was exploding with laughter, gasping with the memory of their blundering agitation. Jim's deeper snorts of mirth joined hers until the truck shook with their uncontrollable laughter. Finally she stopped, wiping at her eyes with the back of her hand. But they looked at each other and it started again, swelling and growing and overtaking them until they were completely spent. They sat quietly then, laughter still creeping over their faces but finished now, only the remnants left. After a few minutes Jim started the truck and turned it around. They drove home silently along the serene, deserted road, the laughter between them like a glowing presence.

In her yard they sat again, unwilling to split that shimmering thing. And she was quiet for the first time in so long, sitting there with her side against the hard, cold door and him behind the wheel just sitting, waiting. She stirred at last, put her hand on the door handle. "Well . . ."

"Wait," he said. In the darkness she could hardly see his face; it floated ghostly and removed from her. He hesitated, then spoke softly, so softly it was almost a whisper and she had to bend toward him to hear. "Are you sure you're okay? You're not upset about it?"

"No," she whispered back at him, stilled. "I'm not."

"Okay."

She waited.

"Judy?"

"What?"

"Can I still call you Judy?"

"Yes." She waited again but he said nothing more, did not reach to touch her. She bit her lip, wanting to feel the warmth of the hand that had gripped her arm so hard in the bar but unable to reach for it herself. Finally she opened the door and went up her sidewalk to the dark house.

He turned the truck around, but stopped while she was still putting her key in the door. "Hey, Judy!" he shouted above the idling motor.

She turned. "What?"

"I love you." And his voice floated to her, mocking and derisive.

"You're crazy!" she yelled at his retreating taillights.

Ten

In Judith's yellow-painted kitchen Mina turned the mug of coffee between her hands. Winter sunlight made the room unbearably bright, forced its brash way into all the corners. "Boy," said Mina, eyes crinkling, "have you ever got yourself a reputation!"

"I can't imagine what for," she said, pulling out a kitchen chair and sitting down opposite Mina. "I didn't do anything."

"Except pick a fight with a bar full of men."

"I didn't. I didn't start it."

Mina chuckled. "You finished it."

"I guess we did at that. Jim helped some."

"Well, it was his fault for taking you into that stinking place anyway."

"Oh, he was the one who got me out of it again. He practically dragged me out the door. Pretty well rescued me."

"He oughtn't to have taken you there in the first place. The same guys in there day after day watching their beer bellies grow and telling the same old stories over and over again. They see a nice-looking young girl come in and they won't let the chance slip by."

"Yeah, I thought they must be kinda bored or they wouldn't have started picking on my pigs."

"They're bored for sure. Nuisance that he is, thank goodness Ed doesn't spend his time in there. I'd sooner he was in front of the TV watching the hockey game."

"Oh well." She picked up Mina's cup and her own and went to the stove to refill them. "You should've seen it. It was kinda funny afterwards."

"I wish I'd have been there. I would have died watching those men heaped up and cowering in front of you."

"They weren't cowering."

"Jim said they were."

"Nah, they were just drunk."

"Well, now you're the Amazon woman of Norberg."

Judith snorted. "Some Amazon."

"You know . . ." Mina stirred sugar into her coffee. "The story will grow and grow and grow." The corners of her mouth twitched. "Pretty soon you'll have fought off the whole bar with your bare hands!"

Judith giggled. "Great. Can't you see me striding down the street with everyone looking after me and saying, 'That's the woman who can fight twenty guys at one time.' "

Mina laughed. "What a reputation! Judith Pierce, the fastest woman in the West."

"And what about my reputation?" She was angry, angry at him for his assumption of her agreement. "I'm the one who feels guilty about it all the time."

"Well, that's your problem. You don't have to."

"Thanks."

He reached for her hand. "Look, Judith, I don't understand. Why does it bother you so much all of a sudden? You said you don't want to get married."

"Because it's so deceptive, so, so . . ."

"Well, what should I do, announce it to the office?"

"No, forget it," she said, and there was weariness in her voice, a bowing to the inevitability of it, the knowledge that she would have to carry her mad plan through, would have to face her unavoidable reparation and escape. She wished for him to take it out of her hands, to sweep her into a plan of his own so that she could abandon hers like the madness it was and so block out the shape of her father's face, stern in death as it had never been in life. For it was his plan, after all, his design, and somewhere he must be watching her pain. *To my only daughter, Judith, I bequeath all my worldly goods, for her to use in remembrance of me.*

That strange phrase in the middle of the legalistic jargon, a quick thrust that left her blind and gasping for a moment, the lawyer's voice hesitating, then, "Aren't you feeling well, Miss Pierce?"

"Yes," she said faintly. "Go on." She felt it too then, a seventy-year-old man and she but twenty-one and his daughter, his daughter.

"Reputation," she said to Mina, stirring her coffee. "What do I care what they think? And funny," she added thoughtfully, "I see some of those guys in the post office every morning and they still don't say one word to me."

"Bar's the only place they can talk."

"They just look down at their feet and talk about the weather."

"Well, they can't very well talk about you when you're standing there, can they?"

"No, but they pretend they don't even know who I am."

Mina shrugged. "Typical. But they'll still tell stories about you."

Her mother thumped the bread dough with her fist. "You should be careful, Judy. You'll get a bad reputation if you don't treat Norman nicer."

"Nice, nice," she raged. "Why can't he be nice and leave me alone! I'm tired of him."

"Well, dear, you should have thought of that before you started to go steady with him."

"Huh . . ." Her father thrust his head into the kitchen. "Leave her be. Don't listen to what anybody says, Judy. Let them talk."

"But he's a nice boy," her mother objected, "and Judy shouldn't just dump him."

"Nice, well, that's one thing, but if she doesn't want to go out with him anymore, why should she?"

"See," she raged, "see? I hate him. He's a dope." And she ran upstairs, slamming the stairway door behind her.

"Well, if they can't talk about me," she said to Mina, "they'll talk about someone else. So why should I care?"

"Speaking of gossip," Mina said. "I'm going to gossip on my own family. I think I'm finally getting rid of one of my sons."

"Oh?" She sat very still, fiddling with her coffee mug and refusing to look at Mina.

"Yes, I think he's finally decided to get married. About time too! Now if I can get rid of the other two soon . . ."

"Which one?" Her voice was soft and frail against Mina's.

"Which one? Oh—John. He's been going out with this girl for so long, I thought he'd never get around to it."

She was alive again. She could look at Mina and breathe. "Are they going to farm?"

"Yes. John owns a quarter already and I think he'll try to buy another one."

"When are they getting married?"

"In the spring—still a ways away, thank goodness." She sipped her coffee meditatively, then grinned. "Say, you wouldn't like to marry Jim to get him off my hands, would you?"

"No."

"Sorry," Mina said quickly. "Only teasing. You're crazy if you do. He hasn't been pestering you, has he?"

"No, he's been very nice."

"I was surprised when he said he was taking you out that night."

"So was I." She laughed. "It's okay, Mina, I can take care of myself."

"Well, you sure are better than those high school girls he's always hanging around with. Too old for their age and one of these days one of them's gonna mean trouble."

"I think he can take care of himself too."

"Hah. Maybe. They are so stupid sometimes I can hardly believe it. Oh well, enough gossip for one morning." Mina shoved back her chair. "I'd better get home before they're all tracking snow into the house."

"Thanks for coming." She held Mina's coat for her. "The day seems to go so much quicker."

"It's nice to come over here and talk." She stamped into her boots. "Hey, when are you coming over to my house?"

Judith hesitated. "Well, a couple of my sows should be coming in pretty soon and I don't know when I can get away . . ."

Mina pursed her lips. "I live just down the road and you coming over for coffee some morning is not going to hurt your blessed pigs."

"It's still hard for me to tell when they're coming in and I'd hate to lose any."

Mina snorted. "Excuses. Don't be so scared of my sons. They're only men. After all, you're coming to visit me, not them."

She had to laugh at Mina's indignant face. "I will. Later this week."

"Okay." Mina pulled open the door and stepped outside. "See you then. Thanks for coffee." The door slammed, then it opened again and Mina poked her head through the crack. "You'll spend Christmas with us anyway," she said. "You can't stay by yourself."

She stood at the window and watched Mina drive away, a dark splotch against the glittering snow. How did she know? The two of them now, Mina and Jim, mother and son, one on either side of her, touching and guiding her as if she were blind. And she felt blind then, rejecting and at the same time holding their reassurance against her lonely isolation in that shimmering expanse of white, her crossing from the house to the barn and back again, pig shit and feed and water and clean straw.

But crossing so often she felt it becoming a ritual and then almost a pleasure, the icy air on her face every morning and the snow crackling under the soles of her rubber boots, the two magpies swooping a few yards away. She hurried to be outside and was sorry to have to go in again, yet refused to stay in the cold without a reason. Afraid of the snow's chill invitation, she plodded from house to barn and barn to house, trying to ignore its icy sensuality, a sensuality that she dispersed on them inside the barn, the folds of her coat emanating a chill with every movement.

Three sows were ready to come in any moment and her trips between house and barn grew steadily more often, the door flying open any time of the night or day to admit her resilient and impatient body, waiting for birth, for action, for one more mark on her private wall, her personal measure.

Coming in one night at eleven before she went to bed, she found one of the sows with four piglets already and a second sow grinding her teeth together in pain. She stayed with them all night, moving from one pen to the other and back, the two litters balancing her restlessness.

The air in the barn hummed with the vibrations of her arms and legs, her voice singing, lifting itself over their sleeping consciousness with a low and comforting resonance. She named the sows Circe and Venus, and she sang all night, her voice rising and falling in measured cadences while she rubbed newborn piglets with straw and thrust them under the heat lamp to dry, while she forked wet straw into the empty wheelbarrow, while she snapped pointed teeth. She fed them then in the early morning, still singing, and when the door closed behind her the thin, high sound of her voice floated back to them, ghostly and content over those frozen dunes of drifts.

She came to the barn even more after that, spent half the day with them. She was starting to feed the oldest piglets hard little pellets of grain and molasses that they chewed half-heartedly, preferring still their mother's hot, sweet milk.

In the mornings she went to town and sometimes to Mina's, but the afternoons were theirs, the rhythm dependable and unbroken. She sang for them often now. And she moved between the house and the barn more easily, finding a sudden exhilaration in the cold; thought of excuses to run to the house and back, her feet ringing on the frozen ground, the snow beneath them a song. The cold invaded her, seduced her.

Throwing back the covers on the bleak and colorless mornings, she caught a light but definite scent in the bedclothes, an odor of skin and sweat and hair and body, and was shocked to rediscover it as her own smell, naked and as pleasing as the snow. So long since she had smelled herself, Judy huddled under the sheets and smelling her small, hard body, an animal's emanation, clear and bitter. Judith smelling like bath oil and too-sweet perfume and makeup and soap and cigarettes and semen, that sharp crease of a man's come redolent and overriding, so there was no secret of her own left, nothing but a frowsy and unclean mustiness coating her skin.

And so she delighted now in the scent of her own purity, rubbed her skin with her hands and smelled them, passed them over her face, threw back her head and stretched her naked body full-length, fingers to the ceiling, in front of the open window. She shrugged into her jeans and sweater as if they were a skin or a pelt, an extension of her alive and breathing skin, unsullied. And she extended it to the pigs, her hands stroking their rough hides, her words like music in their huge, pointed ears.

She felt her body hard and clean and thin under her clothes, felt it chaste and voluptuous, ridding itself of her intemperate indulgence and submission, unlike Judith climbing stairs in a losing battle against her thickening waistline, food and alcohol, tasting stale tobacco on her thick and furry tongue every morning. She sensed the days trickling through her fingers and wanted to shout, Stop, stop, bring them back, I'm not ready yet. Avoiding herself in the mirror, always facing it dressed and under the concealment of clothes. And him, hanging heavy and ugly and overburdened with himself, rubbing his breath, his spit, on her face, his mouth devouring, she felt her skin under it grow gray and papery. And wanted him away, out of her, her vagina clenched tight as a purse string, his lumpish body so cumbersome she waited only for the time when she could be alone.

Layer by layer she shed the accumulation of those years, the thickness between herself and her surface growing smaller and smaller each day until she could feel through her skin the push of bones, their angular fragility. And she lost her stiffness, the jerky awareness that had carved her movements for so long, fluid and shapely she slid around the pigs, moved between them like a sorceress.

In town one Saturday afternoon for bread and milk she passed Jim going the other way, a curly blonde head close beside him in the truck. And in the store, paying for her purchases, was surprised to find him standing beside her.

"Hey, Judy." His eyes were as mischievous as always. "Wanna bust up the bar tonight?"

"Sorry, I'm busy." She dug into her pocket for some change. "Besides, you've got company."

He shrugged. "I'm just giving her a ride. I keep waiting for you to invite me over, but you never do."

"Do I have to invite you? Seems to me you invited yourself last time."

"Well, after watching that episode in the bar, I don't want to get on your bad side."

"Jim." She turned to him, picking up her bag of groceries. "If you make your friend wait in the truck, she's going to get awfully cold. It's twenty below."

He grinned and followed her out. "Hey, Judy?"

She was getting into her own truck, her back turned to him. "What?"

"See you tonight."

She didn't answer, only slammed the truck door.

He came at nine o'clock, first tooting his horn and then knocking a tattoo on the door.

"Go away," she said, "I'm busy."

His eyes swept the kitchen. "Playing solitaire. I thought you were busy."

"I am."

"Let me help you then." He kicked off his overshoes. "Blackjack's better."

She played him for pennies, hostile and silent. Finally, dealing and flipping cards at him angrily, he caught her wrist. "Judy." She sat perfectly still, staring at him. "Look, it's a game. It's a joke to take those kids out."

"Then why don't you bother them instead of me?"

"Because you're better."

She twisted away from him and dealt again. "It's your business. I don't care."

"And we're gonna be friends?"

She looked down, nodded, hiding it, the thick swell of her desire waiting every time she looked at him.

"Hah," he said. "Twenty-one. I win."

And he came often now, sometimes before she was through with the pigs in the barn, and he would stand in the aisle and talk and laugh while she finished watering and scattering fresh straw in the pens.

"Hey, Judy. These piglets are getting big. You're gonna have to wean them pretty soon."

"I know," she said. "Get away from that fence, you fool, or Marie Antoinette will eat your arm."

"Hey, and you know what else? You've gotta castrate these pigs, Judy, or they'll be so big you can't hold them down."

"I know. After Christmas."

And now each time he came he made her repeat the names until it became a kind of litany or ritual. She would say the name and point out the sow and he would repeat it until finally he could chant them with her: "Marie Antoinette Josephine Daisy Emily Circe Venus and Annie." Then they would laugh until the pigs were grunting and squealing and the air in the barn rang with their combined gratification.

He came to know them well; would scratch behind an ear or bend from the waist toward the whoofing snout of one of the sows. And when he came they snorted and grunted an exhilarated welcome; the smell of them together—he and Judith—was an unbearable pleasure to them.

She never failed to inform him, "You're disturbing my pigs!" But he laughed all the louder and they whoofed and scrambled harder.

"Lady," he said, "you slop pigs beautifully."

And she spent Christmas with them, his noise and Mina's smile blocking out her father's quiet voice and rough face still cold from the morning chores when he carried her down the stairs in her blue-flowered nightgown, still half asleep against his shoulder until she saw the lighted tree.

Lilith's piglets were born between Christmas and New Year's, and that night he stayed with her, sitting on a straw bale in the hush of the barn, strangely quiet and subdued himself.

"Hey, Judy," he said softly.

"What?" She was bent over a newborn piglet, massaging him with straw.

"These are spooky animals, you know."

"Why?"

"Because you think they're sleeping and you go and look and their eyes are open." He listened for a moment. "And their eyes are red."

She laughed softly. "Of course. They're supernatural. Whatever made you think I'd have ordinary pigs?"

"It's not a joke, it's real. They're always awake."

"I know." She rubbed her hands with straw and sat back on her heels, looking up at him.

"It's you. You're a witch. Somebody's gonna find out and burn you."

She looked at him, so wild and gentle, and

she thought he must be able to see it, the hot fluid ache that ran always under her surface for him. But he turned his head to listen to the rustle of quiet breathing surrounding them, and she stood awkward and rough. "I'm crazy, that's all."

When he came they played cribbage, they listened to the radio, they drank vodka and orange juice. Sometimes they went skating at the rink in town. She even tried to curl with him, then told him it was a ridiculous game, sweeping the ice with a broom in front of a rock. Good way to throw your back out.

And always she waited, waited for him to touch her like she had never had to wait for anyone, so stiff and resistant in her waiting that he waited too, sensing the clenched anxiety of her body and not knowing what it meant or whether he dared approach her.

Finally she decided she had to hold something out, had to broach him somehow. He was leaning back in his chair, hands behind his head, after beating her at cribbage five times. "Well, I guess I better get home."

She licked her lips, went to stand at the window, facing the darkness. "Are you afraid of me?"

Startled, he glanced at her. "Afraid of you? Why?"

She shrugged. "I don't know."

He laughed then. "You bet I'm afraid of you. You're a scary lady."

"You're so careful." She was serious.

"That's easy." And she knew that he had slipped around her again. "You're clean, Judy. You're the cleanest woman, no, person, I've ever seen in this muddy place. Maybe because you're so sure about what you don't want."

She said nothing, still facing that mirror-like window, reflecting her tired mouth and the anxious corners of her eyes.

"I guess that's why I call you Judy. You sometimes seem so much like a serious little kid."

My little girl Judy, come here, come to daddy, you are so pretty, you are my little girl, give me a tight hug, you won't go away from daddy and the farm, I will always take care of you.

"I'm twenty-three," she said.

He laughed. "Hey, so am I." He came to stand behind her at the window, watched her in that inverted mirror, then put his hands on her shoulders. She could feel her bones under the light weight of his fingers, pliant and eager for him to crush them in a hard grasp. "Don't think so much," he said. "I'm going now."

And standing like that he bent and brushed his cheek against her hair in a movement so quick and unexpected she was frozen, could not reach to touch him, and then he was no longer behind her but at the door, donning his coat. She watched him tie the laces of his boots, the quick gestures of his long fingers like a flagrant display of his sexuality. Hand on the doorknob, he turned to her and winked. "Take care of those pigs, Judy."

She had to smile at him. "I will, don't worry."

On Sundays she would walk with her father, hand lost in his, down the dirt machinery path to the back quarter hill high above the rest of the land. Running his hand over the tops of the green wheat—he would break off a stalk and look at it, slowly and absorbed, while she drew patterns in the dust with her black leather Sunday shoes. The path looped around the sloughs in slow curves that she loved to follow, scuffing her newly polished toes in the dust. At the top of the hill they stood and gazed at the green sea of wheat, then turned and looked at the white house, the red pig barns beyond it long and low. Reluctantly they stood, knowing that now they would have to go back, walk down the hill instead of up. Her father turned. "Guess it's time to go back, Judy. Pretty soon time for tea." In some places the grain grew higher than her head and he carried her on his shoulders. You are my little girl, my only little girl, this is all for you, and she felt his shoulders under the heat of her legs, thick and strong and warm, and before he put her down he hugged her against him, her body tight and close to his chest, her bones almost crushed in his arms.

Feeding the pigs the next morning Judith swore and kicked an empty water pail down the aisle. She stomped to retrieve it and grabbed at the edge of the pail, not noticing a ragged tear in the aluminum from the strain of the handle. Her hand flashed instant fire and she pulled it away with a gasp as a spurt of blood welled from the base of her thumb across her wrist. Clutching the cut hand with the other she ran to the chorehouse to hold it under the cold-water tap.

The water stained red and blood swelled from the edge of her wrist. She felt herself sway, the gray outlines of the chorehouse around her spinning. Quickly she squatted, put her head between her knees until the blackness receded, then still holding her bleeding hand she threw her coat over her shoulders and ran to the half-ton. She unplugged the block heater and started it on the third try, then drove in second gear with one hand on the wheel and the other dripping blood onto her coat.

They were quiet, sensing her pain and outrage, her somehow self-inflicted injury. Anxious and restive they waited for her to return.

She was in Mina's yard before she realized that she was crying and trembling. Her knees buckled when she climbed out of the truck so that she knelt in the snow, and the trickle of blood from her hand dyed the rough white particles red. Mina was suddenly beside her, coatless and anxious.

"I . . . I cut my hand on a water pail."

Mina was turning her hand upwards, looking at the ragged gash. ". . . blood poisoning," Judith heard her say.

"I have to go back and finish watering the pigs." The yard was so white, so dazzlingly white.

"You're not going anywhere." Somehow she felt herself standing on that slippery snow, felt Mina's smaller body hauling her toward the house like an awkward sack of feed.

Inside, Mina put her hand into a basin of cold water with baking soda, then wrapped the still-bleeding cut tightly. "Now you lie right here on the couch," she said. "It doesn't look bad enough to go to the doctor. We'll see if it stops bleeding."

In the morning stillness of Mina's house there was only the sound of water running and dishes banging. Judith thought of that first night she had been here for supper, and now the house was almost as familiar as her own. She looked up at the ceiling, suddenly feeling peaceful and sleepy. The pigs could wait for a while.

Judy lay on the living room couch with the quilt tucked under her feet and the bottle of red pills on the coffee table beside her. Her mother sang in the kitchen.

"Sleep," her mother said. "You have to sleep if you want to get better, Judy."

"But it's daytime. I'm not sleepy."

"Then just lie quietly."

The clock went ticktock, ticktock. Maybe Daddy would come in for coffee soon. Ticktock. The clock was noisy. She turned on her side and put her hand under her cheek, staring at the green weave of the upholstery. A million tiny squares in one inch. The door banged open and she felt a gust of wind whoosh through the house. She sat up on the couch. "Daddy?"

He came to her quickly, still in his overcoat, and picked her up to hold her against him, so cold and red his face.

"James, you're all cold. You'll make her sicker."

But he clutched her tighter, wrapped the quilt around her as close and muffled as a mummy, and he carried her to the kitchen and held her while he drank his morning coffee, careful not to put his cold face too close to her but holding her against him so tightly, as if he would pour all his thick, hard life into her, white and pale and wrapped in the quilt.

Opening her eyes she found him standing beside the couch in a pair of stained jeans and a blue shirt open at the neck.

"Judy," he said. "I'm beginning to think you're violent. First you pick a fight in the bar, then you try to cut your hand off!"

Sleeves rolled up to his elbows, fine, dark hairs showed along the edge of his arm and up to his wrist.

She struggled into a sitting position; lying on her back to look up at him made her feel helpless and vulnerable. "That pail attacked me!" she said cheerfully.

He grinned. "I'll bet. Hey, Mom says do you want some lunch."

She swung her legs over the edge of the couch. "I have to get home."

"Nah, I went and finished feeding your pigs."

"What?"

"What do you think I am, a dummy? I've watched you do it so many times I could do it with my eyes closed. Come and have lunch."

Her hand had stopped bleeding but she stayed the afternoon with Mina, drinking tea in the bright, blue kitchen.

"I'm tired of winter," Mina said. "After Christmas everything goes downhill until spring comes. I can hardly wait to get out and putter around in the garden."

"Yes," Judith said. "And I'll have to buy a boar at the spring sale."

"And John will get married, I suppose." She hesitated perceptibly. "Judy, Jim isn't bothering you, is he?"

"No, we get along fine."

"I guess I worry about it. I don't want my crazy son to get in the way of our friendship."

She touched Mina's hand with her bandaged one. "Don't worry." They sat quietly for a moment. "It's just nice to have a male around. And he's pleasant and he's quite attractive, you know."

"Oh I know," said Mina, the smile trembling on the edges of her lips. "You can't do with them and you can't do without them. I just don't want him to fool around with you."

They sat looking at each other and then Judith started to laugh and after a moment Mina joined her, saying, "What is it? What's so funny?"

"It's crazy," Judith said. "I'd like to get him into bed, but he's so scared of me he won't come near me. That's my punishment, I guess. He always leaves really fast as if he's afraid that I'm going to suggest something immoral."

Mina shook with laughter. "Boy, that's a new one for him. You must have really scared him because I don't think he's ever bothered to keep his hands off a woman yet."

They rocked back and forth in their chairs until Mina finally gasped, "Maybe you could pay him."

They both howled. "Oh sure," said Judith, "and get him to feed the pigs on top of it." Gradually they subsided but they could not help smiling at each other like conspirators. "Just don't you put any ideas in his head," Judith warned.

"Don't worry," Mina giggled.

They did not notice the darkness creeping over the afternoon until the men came stomping in for supper.

"Hey, I have to go home. My pigs will be screaming."

"Gab, gab, gab, that's all you women ever do," Ed said.

Mina looked at Judith's hand again. "I think it'll be fine, but you'll have to wear a bandage and keep it clean. You better come over in a couple of days so I can change it. You won't be able to with one hand."

"All right." She hurried down the walk and turned to wave her unhurt hand at them, standing there in the doorway. "See you and thanks a lot."

"See you yourself," Jim said behind her. "How're you gonna do your chores like that?"

"Easy. Same's I do everything else by myself."

He looked at her above the turned-up collar of his overcoat. "Yeah, I'll bet you will." He winked and opened her truck door. "Allow me." When she was behind the wheel he leaned into the cab and whispered to her, "Hey, lady, can you ever slop pigs!"

"Go away," she said, smiling at him. "Clean out your own barn first."

Eleven

The two magpies seemed determined to outlast the winter with her. Through the window she watched them every morning as they hopped about the yard, head at an inquisitive angle and beady eyes fixed. When the wind blew they vanished, but in the sunshine the yard was their domain and they patrolled it thoroughly. Raucous and harlequin though they were, she even came to like them, shook her crumbs out for them so that now whenever she opened the door they cocked their heads from whatever perch they occupied and squawked at her.

She still heard the coyotes but sporadic and far away, the distance lessening their uneasy keening to a sound that blended into the winter wind.

She went to Norberg every day now. That had become a ritual for her too, the drive to and from town over the snow-plowed roads, until finally she knew every crack and bump, knew when to expect the lurch of the wheel under her hands. Faces in the town were becoming distinguishable. Some of them even nodded at her when she entered the stuffy post office lobby to stand waiting for the mail to be sorted and the wicket to rattle open. Now she didn't have to tell the postmaster her name, but he still said nothing to her, silently thrusting the few envelopes across the counter or simply shaking his head.

She knew they talked her over between themselves, weighing her folly. Not that she cared much. The Stambys' acceptance, especially Jim's, made her existence an indisputable and not-to-be-shrugged-off fact. But still, when she shoved open the door to the dark and musty interior of the creaky-floored grocery store, she could not help knowing that everyone stopped talking and followed her progress among the shelves with curious eyes.

Mina was right, she had become a story to them, a madwoman. Someone would even invariably say hello, but still they watched her covertly, expecting some flamboyant act, disappointed when she did not fling jars and cans as they had heard she flung beer. And when the door slammed behind her with her small bag of butter and tea, only the essentials, she could not help but hear them, or at least imagine that she did.

"Boy, who does she think she is, anyway?"

"Crazy as a hoot owl."

"I'll say. Livin' with a bunch of pigs."

"Ah, she'll never make it. These city people. She'll quit, just wait and see."

She gritted her teeth and slammed the door of the half-ton. Now if she was someone's wife it would be different. Then they would have been full of praise—a marvelous woman helping her husband to do everything, working just as hard as he did.

But in the mirror at night before she went to bed, she saw herself as they must see her, green eyes that were gathering tiny wrinkles, short brown hair, a medium-sized, slightly pretty woman in her middle twenties, always wearing blue jeans and with an edge of dirt under her fingernails, a crazy lady who liked mucking out pigs better than typing legalistic letters with clean hands and polished fingernails. And she would laugh soundlessly at herself, laugh and clap her hands and shake her fist at the obedient image.

In the barn the pigs waited for her to turn on the light in the mornings before they rustled out of their nests. They squealed and snorted when they heard the rattle of the pails. And she was relaxed and easy now. Even after slashing her hand on the pail she came to them with an open impulsiveness that was almost sensual, her body bending and genuflecting in the push and lift of the pitchfork and shovel, presiding over the water she poured from the pails.

Even angry sometimes, she was still grateful for their animal constancy. At night after they had been fed and watered and while they rooted in the crisp, snow-smelling straw, she sometimes sat on a bale or an overturned pail, seeming almost to hold her breath for them. The naked light bulbs overhead gave off a dusty glow and the pigs were a rotund and sturdy contrast to the cobwebs gathered in the corners of the barn. Pugnacious and daring, the piglets fought among themselves in the last of their frantic infancy.

She looked at them over the fence and sighed, counting the weeks on her fingers. Six weeks old and it was time for them to be weaned, to be castrated. Not that they could know or care. It was her worry. And the last two sows had their piglets.

"What are you going to call this one?" Mina asked Judith who was screwing the infrared lamp into the hanging socket.

"I don't know. I've run out of names."

Mina giggled. "I've never had a namesake. Couldn't name my sons after myself."

"You want me to name one of my sows after you?" Judith turned from the lamp to look at Mina with a quizzical smile.

Mina shrugged. "Why not? I'm not proud."

For a long moment they looked at one another, those two women, caught in their complicity like lovers or children who have started a fire together. "I'd love it, as long as you don't mind." Judith's smile lit up her face, her eyes crinkling and slanted with happiness.

"Would I suggest it if I was going to mind? Come on, Judy, let's christen her!"

"Wait," said Judith. "Then I'll call the last one Judith after myself."

Mina laughed. "Why not? You deserve some credit."

Judith rushed to the fence and hugged her, holding Mina's body against her own. And when they broke apart their faces were no longer laughing, but still and frightened, as if they had seen too much of something.

Judith's lips started to form words but Mina held up her hand, wouldn't let her say them. "Don't," she said. "You'll make me cry." They were quiet for a long time.

"They'll be the best sows of all," Judith said softly. "Mina and Judith. I know it."

And she had even come to like her house, the small rooms, the awkward angles. Now she carried the warmth from the barn with her into the house and it caught there and seemed to grow a little every day, like the pigs did, eating and sleeping and playing in the barn.

After she cut her hand, Jim came over every night, not wanting her to use it; and he carried pails for her until Mina let her take the bandage off.

The piglets stood, noses raised to him while he poured water into their mother's trough.

"Judy, these pigs are gigantic. How old are they?"

"Seven weeks."

"Aren't you going to wean them?"

"Yeah, I better."

"Where are you gonna put them?"

"Well, I'll put two of the sows together and then put the weaners all in one pen."

"Don't you think the sows will jump these fences if the weaners scream enough?"

"I don't think so. The weaners have been eating those pellets pretty good lately. I think it'll only be a day or so before they're used to it."

"And then what?"

She looked at him. "What do you mean?"

"Well, aren't you going to breed the sows again?"

"Yes, I'll just give them a rest while I look for a boar. I guess it's about time I did."

"Where are you gonna put him?"

"Well, the corral's all right because I fixed it in the fall, but there's no shelter. I'll have to put up a shed or something. That's not really a problem. What's worse is that I have to castrate these weaners."

"Yeah, they're pretty big."

Judith looked at him but he said nothing, only whistled and grinned at her.

"Damn you," she said finally. "You only offer to help when I don't need you. I've managed to do everything myself until now."

He laughed. "You're so prickly, Judy. I just wanted to see if you would actually come out and ask me to help. Look, I'll come and do it with Jerry or John tomorrow."

"Oh no, they're my pigs, I can help you. I just can't do it all by myself."

"Okay, sure. Have you got everything you need? Dettol, a scalpel, bunch of clean rags?"

"Yes. And I'll pay you."

"What for?"

"For your services as a hired man."

"Ah, forget it, Judy. I was only teasing when I said I wanted to see if you'd really ask me. Come on, I'll bet I can beat you to the house."

And they were gone, winking the barn into darkness and leaving the mingled smell of their human oppositeness behind them. The pigs snuffled in the straw and stretched on their sides, peaceful and serene, their breathing a rising and falling motion in the darkness, secure and unapprehensive.

But they knew instinctively the next morning, Judith coming to the barn with him instead of going to town for the mail; a heap of white rags and a shiny instrument, carrying with them a cold carbolic smell of disinfectant that rose from the two pails of hot water still steaming from the freezing air outside.

"How are we gonna do this?" Jim asked. "If we cut them in the aisle, the sows are liable to go crazy."

"We'll put a couple of straw bales in the chorehouse and do it there." Judith was already hauling them in from the stack outside. She put one of them across the other in the shape of a T, put one water pail and the rags on the bale then said, "Okay."

They could not know that the shiny instrument was for their testicles; that this part of her plan was as terrible as their birth had been wonderful, that for the males among them her next step was emasculation.

"Since the sows are used to me, I guess I should catch them. Don't want you to get bitten," she said, grinning at him. She was taking off her coat and rolling up her shirt sleeves, the pale curve of her throat behind her open collar glinting luminous in the light filtering through the windows.

"Fine by me," Jim said. "I'll bet the little buggers don't want to be caught."

Inside the pen she stood for a minute while

they scrambled around and over her too-big boots, as they always did, snorting and mock-fighting.

"These are mostly males too," she said.

He came and stood beside the pen so that the smell of them, her cold smell of snow and his hot smell of earth, mingled. The piglets cocked their heads up at him. "Hey, Judy, look, if you don't want to do it, I'll just get John or Jerry to help me."

"Don't be silly. When I was thirteen I helped the vet do an emergency Caesarian section on a sow. Can you imagine what that was like? We did it in my father's barn and we had to tie her upside down! This is nothing." She neglected to tell him that she had never even seen a pig castrated.

She stooped swiftly and her small, hard hand flashed. In an instant she was holding one of the weaners by a hind leg. She stood and held him upside down, squealing and struggling against the firm grip on his leg and his upturned world; then easily swung the pig and herself over the fence and carried him down the aisle to the chorehouse.

"You hold him," Jim said, "and I'll cut."

She swung the helpless weaner onto his back on the straw bale and knelt over him, held him tight between her knees while she grasped both his hind legs.

Jim wrung one of the rags out in the disinfected water and firmly wiped the pig's genitals. Between her knees he shrilled and struggled, unused to lying on his back and suddenly desperately afraid but unable to move, held there by her knees, her hands.

Picking up the scalpel, Jim weighed it in his hand, looking down at the two bulbs of the testicles, still young and firm and unwrinkled.

"Come on," she said. "This little bugger is slippery."

Quiet in concentration, he bent over the pig. Laying his hand on the belly he carefully sliced down the division between the two halves, pulling the skin open, slicing them out, the purple testicles under a well of blood. The pig squealed and wriggled frantically as he flicked the blue, crushed-grape lobes onto the floor. "Okay."

She released the pig from between her knees and carried him back to the pen, still squalling and shuddering under her grasp. The sows whoofed and snorted in a frenzy, lathering themselves into fury at the weaner's cries. And she said nothing to them, did not speak to soothe them but simply released the pig in the pen and picked up another. And then they knew, could all of them already feel the prick and then the thin, sharp slice of that knife on their sex, ripping into them and disemboweling the very heart of their nature. Not even Circe's turning men to swine could equal it.

She swung that pig over the fence and carried him to the chorehouse through the whoofing cries of the sows. She flung him on the bale and held him down grimly, lip caught between her teeth and face set.

Holding the scalpel, Jim looked at her tight and drained face. "Judy," he said.

"Come on, come on." She was impatient and furious, trapped by what she sensed was her betrayal of the pigs.

He bent over the piglet again, silent, laid the blade against that line of skin dividing the two testicles. Slicing, he was awkward and the cut was not clean and deep but a swipe at the surface nerves, the pig desperately trying to draw his hindquarters away from that slash at his genitals; if he could have drawn them up into himself he would have and suffered death rather than have them touched. But no, the man was slicing again, another clumsy sawing cut that drew a shrill scream from the bottom of the pig's throat and left the others in the pen silent and terrorized.

"For God's sake, Jim," she said. "Come on!"

He said nothing, cut again and finally exposed those blue lobes, perfect and irridescent, swirled with color and veins, almost marbled. If you bit into one of them, she thought, they would be crunchy, they would have the grainy texture of apples. He sliced quickly but clumsily, hacking at the glistening fruit hidden in the scrotum, drawing lines of blood while the pig squirmed.

Finally, finally, her body cramped and panting with tight resentment, she could carry the pig back to the pen. She flung him down and he staggered away from her, the squeals gradually dying in his throat.

Then she picked up the next one. He did not squeal. The floor swung beneath his snout as she carried him by his right hind leg to the chorehouse, flung him on his back on that butcher's straw bale. Breathless, he did not struggle, even knowing what was going to happen. There were whirling shapes, the movement of two human bodies on the periphery of his vision, the smell of her skin and clothes; even with the scent of blood on her hands, she still smelled like snow.

She held him there and stared at Jim holding that shiny and now red-edged scalpel. And he looked back at her for a moment with a kind of despair in his eyes; and now she knew why he never touched her, why there was always the distance between them. That sudden knowledge flashed on her. I wanted too much, she thought. I have always wanted too much and not enough, and why can I not just let things go, let them be and allow them to go on?

She reached out her hand, now sure and fearless, so perfectly knowing. "Give me that thing and you hold this pig down." She shifted and the piglet felt her weight transfer, felt heavier bones settle over him. And then she was wiping his scrotum with a warm, strong-smelling wet cloth, and then there was the slice, quick and clean, the piglet's furious shriek on the heels of it, Judith slicing at the membranes of his testicles while he fought away from her knife, wriggling and squealing. And she slipped them out of him so easily, so swiftly presiding over his emasculation like the savage witch of pragmatism that she was.

Perhaps it was atonement for the acts of barbarity she had committed on herself for him: plucking her sleek eyebrows, rolling her straight hair into curls, thrusting golden posts through the holes in her ears. Did all that and then resented his acceptance of it as his due, his casual, "You look lovely tonight, Judith." She knew that they would stay with her, those indentations, those marrings of her pale and pliant flesh, so that even the silken edge of hair along the skin of her arm was unnatural, somehow perverse. And still she could not quarry her response to him, could not lay bare that vehement craving and cut it out. Recognized too late the change he had orchestrated in her, the loss of her unstudied awkwardness resulting from his sandpaper polishing, his careful honing of her salient features into his special mold. And then she was ashamed.

She castrated them all. Swift and cruel she pierced them, slicing so fast there was hardly time for blood to flow, flicking their testicles onto the floor of the chorehouse like offending parasites.

Jim held them silently, sweating, his eyes averted from hers in some other icy cast of fear. She could almost have asked him to lie down on that bale, had she done it with the same coolness and finesse that she tackled them, she who had never before held that blade in her hand, her father always hiring a neighbor to help, refusing even when she was eighteen to let her near the barn while they were castrating. Perhaps he did not want her to witness a male emasculating a male, the castration of his own species, and so saved himself from her discovery of his common humanity, saved himself from her discovery of his own sexuality.

That was how she could immortalize him, could worship and long and ache to have him take her, father and daughter in their complicity, their mutual preservation of the lie, casting themselves forever on the mercy of their ideal. And so it was that she could love him, father/god perfect always, unfailing, showing her only birth and death and never the sordid in-between, the soiled and rumpled edges of what the others were so eager, so pleased, to show her. Within that discrepancy she came to hate him and then to idolize him, and then again full circle to her childishness, trying to please him.

Judith making furtive calculations on her telephone memos, writing letters to farm real estate agents on her IBM Selectric, taking a subscription to the hog journal. Adding columns of figures, of legacy and savings, of purchase and mortgage, of output and return, of time and money, her calculated gamble in a double column of figures that balanced and coded her escape and redemption.

It would have been an expiation for her, and for them living in a split-level bungalow in Stettler where her father coughed and paced the floor every morning, finally driving into the country to watch other farmers working in their fields. So she hugged it to herself, saved it, wanted to present it to him whole and ready to carry out, to be able to say to him, her father, "Look, I'll do it. I'll begin like you did and we'll start over. I will, I will."

But she kept it to hersef too long, too late.

She was frying mushrooms so she told him to answer the telephone, pick up the receiver. When he held it toward her, she took the time to remove the pan from the burner, to rinse and dry her hands before she raised the black instrument to hear the disembodied voice that came over the wire.

And it was not the moment or the shock that burned itself into her mind, but her omission. So close, she was almost ready to tell him, to go home to him and say, "Yes, I will." But he was gone, dead, and she had not even told him that she meant to redeem them all, the two of them together again, forever and irrevocably joined.

So this is the way it happens, she thought, holding the telephone receiver in her hand like a weapon. Failing to stop at a stop sign. And she thrust him away from her, his anxious, puzzled face advancing and receding, wrested her rigid body away from his eager consolation, pushing him aside to walk to the bedroom and calmly lay some clothes in a suitcase.

He stood, the only time she saw him helpless, in front of her. "Don't you want me to come with you, Judith?"

"What for?"

"To help you. You can't do all this by yourself."

"How could you help? You'd just get in the way."

"But somebody's got to help you."

She shrugged. "There are neighbors."

"But . . . I can be there, darling. You must be in shock."

"No."

"But, Judith . . ."

She spun around then and lashed at him. "Why in God's name do you want to go with me to arrange and attend a messy funeral? You never even met them. That wasn't in our bargain." She was suddenly screaming at him. "He was *my* father, they were my parents." And then slid under it, the battering onslaught of her pain and pride and frustration, hard, dry sobs that drove themselves against the walls of her body like blows. So that he had his chance, the chance to comfort her in the one moment that she showed herself to him as a child.

And she did it alone. For him and without him. Waited and planned and worked alone. It mattered little whether he was alive or dead, she had to show him that she would hold herself for him, her father.

And now she had seen the core, the axis always unexplained and mysterious, more than a fusion of beginning and end, but the stuff that days and weeks and months are made of, the continual hard, resistant core.

Judith castrated the last pig, then threw down the scalpel and stood erect, stretching tired arms above her head. She plunged her hands into the pail of warm water, blood swirling away from them, then dried them on one of the rags. Sighing deeply, she flung the straw bales out of the barn and into the snow to freeze the stink of blood and fear out of them.

He was standing in the chorehouse pulling on his coat and she could see his breath coming and going hard.

"Come in the house," she said, deadly quiet, "and I'll pay you."

He shook his head. "Sorry, I don't take money for doing nothing."

"I couldn't have done it alone." And she was icily furious with him. "Don't be so stubborn."

"Doesn't matter." And he was gone, out the door and loping long strides to his truck. From the door of the barn she watched him get in and drive away, going too fast and spinning snow from his tires. She shrugged then, feeling the lightness of relief. It was no longer her worry, her problem; she was free.

She went back inside the barn and spoke to the pigs, leaning over the fence and letting her voice, her words, fall onto them as they stood subdued and listening, slaves to a master, Circe's humans.

"Don't be mad," she said. "It had to be done. I'm sorry." And they looked up at her and flicked their ears and blinked their orange eyes.

She stayed with them in the barn all that day, walked up and down the aisle, talking and singing. She scraped up the blackening lobes that were scattered on the chorehouse floor with the shovel and buried them in the manure heap, then swept the floor down with water from the tap, erasing the smell and the sour tension of fear. At four o'clock she cleaned the pigs, fed and watered them, going through the ritual like a reassurance.

Finished, she stood in the center of the barn, quiescent and passive as a bride, a piece of straw caught in her hair, her ears so tidy and white beneath that ragged fringe. And then, having done all she could, her relief faded and she felt again the weight of opprobrium, of anxiety. And even fighting it, it grew, still not expurgated, her savage distaste with herself.

She slammed out of the barn and stamped

up the hill to the house, the monologue beginning again: How can I keep on with this, I won't, I will sell this damn place tomorrow, I'll get a job again, I can't, I can't, I must be crazy, shit and blood and snow when I could be typing letters in soft clothes and with clean hands.

In her darkening house she kicked off her boots but did not even stop to remove her coat. Standing at the kitchen window, she looked out at the ghostly pall of the snow-covered yard. The raucous spectre of a magpie glided by to land on the fence and mock her with the cock of its head. Huddled inside her coat, the barn smell of them still surrounded her. Why do you stay, you don't have to, you are free, they can't keep you here. It's ridiculous, pigs and pigs and pigs. Shoveling shit and carrying feed and water and bloody births and castrating pigs and pigs and pigs for the rest of your life and then what will happen? He's dead anyway and Jim running away like that, it's wrong, it's all wrong. It's too late.

You are my little girl, my only little girl, aren't you, Judy, my little girl, come here, Judy, you little sweetheart, daddy will take care of you and this is all for you, we'll stay together forever and ever.

The magpie flashed by again and she shuddered, shook her head to clear it. She dropped her coat there, by the window, and went to the bathroom, pulled off her clothes as if they were bandages and turned to look full at herself in the mirror. She saw her face white and triangular, her breasts sagging and with a crease of wrinkles around their fullness, her cold skin gray under the light. She was paper, paper dead. She spun the shower taps furiously, then dove in to punish her numb skin under the fierce needles. The water splintered away the smell of them, of their fear, their passionate dependence on her. And in the heat and the water the weight of them subsided a little so that she could almost move freely again.

She rubbed herself dry and on an impulse dabbed some perfume behind her knees. Then kicking aside her barn clothes, she walked naked through the dim and silent house to her bedroom, again the sense that this was more her room than any. Jim had been in the living room and the kitchen but never here, never in her room. And what would she have done if he had wanted her? Acquiesced and resented him for it? She could not know and did not want to, pushed aside the idea as she stood looking, looking for that other Judith.

The clothes hung untouched in the back of her closet, still permeated with the vague aura of dancing and long, sequestered evenings. She reached blindly and her hand touched soft, plush cloth. She pulled it out, the full, rich skirt of midnight-blue velvet hanging from her fingers. Behind it hung a creamy-white silk blouse. She stripped them off the hangers and slipped her body into them, the skirt falling dark and heavy onto her hips and the electric blouse cleaving to her naked breasts. The material felt like touch against her skin, the tips of a man's fingers running over her. The now-unfamiliar skirt flowed behind her through the house and she was suddenly unsure of how to carry herself, where to put her hands.

She stood in the middle of the dark kitchen, upright, her hands folded in front of her, feeling her body under the sweep of the clothes. She took one step and then another, perfectly straight and composed as she had never been when she wore them for others, for him in the city. An alive thing, the skirt folded thick and cool against the muscles of her legs. She moved toward the wall light switch, then hesitated and shrugged, rummaged in her junk drawer, fingers passing through odds and ends—pieces of string, a tin of thumbtacks, a couple of leftover company pens with their ends bitten.

Finally she emerged with a half-burned candle. Fingers awkward, she fumbled with a match. She lit the stub and set it on a saucer in its own warm wax.

You're crazy, she admonished herself. You're crazy. Blow the damn thing out and go to bed. But she found herself suddenly certain and assured, swishing about the kitchen in the trailing skirt. Muscles, she thought, I have muscles. She moved slowly and with reverence, more self-aware than ever. And she thought that she would broil herself a steak, thick and bloody, and have a drink from the half-empty bottle of whiskey she had brought from the city.

Sitting in front of the melting candle, plate centered on a mat and flatware neatly in line, she ate slowly and pleasurably.

Well, here I am where I never expected to be.

But her other self asked, And what did you expect?

I always expect something different from what I get.

Does it make so much difference?

I suppose it shouldn't, but . . .

She held up the glass of golden liquid against the light of the flame.

Will the price of pigs make a difference?

Not anymore.

Abruptly the flame spluttered and died. She sighed. "Here I am in the dark again," she said aloud.

Leaving the dishes on the table, she scraped back her chair and went to sit at the window, gazing at the almost indistinguishable bulk of the barn. She sat quietly, the skirt folding around her ankles and the blouse touching the rise and fall of her breasts. And she didn't even move when his lights swept into the yard and he slammed the truck door. He didn't knock, just opened her door and walked in, and she was relieved, so happy—Jim, James, her father or her non-existent, never-existed, implausible lover.

"Judy?"

"Yes."

He picked his way toward her across the dark kitchen. "Why are you sitting in the dark?"

She said nothing, felt him standing behind her chair, the sharp, clean smell of him cutting into her senses.

"Sorry I took off this morning." His voice fell over her quietly, like warm water.

"That's all right."

"Judy."

"What?"

"You . . . you scared me."

She shrugged.

"You're so damned . . . what is it? . . . indifferent."

"That's a big word. Reminds me of the big words I used to type."

"So what?"

"So nothing."

"Listen," he said, and his voice was low and urgent. "Listen, the way you went at those pigs this morning, how do I know what you'd do to me?"

"You don't."

He stood very still behind her and she felt herself starting to cry—damn, the worst possible thing for her to do. She took a deep breath to stop herself, felt his hand warm on the coolness of her blouse before he pulled it away as if she had bitten him.

"Christ, what have you got on?"

"Clothes."

And she must have given herself away because suddenly he was kneeling beside her and touching her everywhere, hands on her face and down her arms, fingers on her lips and her chin and her throat.

"No," she said.

"Judy, shhh, listen, little girl, don't be so afraid all the time, you're safe now, my little Judy, shhh."

She pushed him away and stood up, straight and tall with that skirt draped down the length of her leg and the thin blouse sticking to her skin. "I'm not little. I'm twenty-three years old. And if you dare to call me Judy, you'll pay."

He laughed. "I dare."

She shrugged. And she didn't even touch him, just walked through the house to her bedroom. And she unbuttoned that blouse and dropped that skirt on the floor without even looking at him leaning in the doorway watching her. And oh yes, it was very good. There was something about denying her childishness that made it better than it had ever been, the length of him inside her shucking away all those years like so much chaff, and she was pounding his back with her fists and in the barn the pigs heard it and knew, her drawnout wail filtering through the wood like the announcement of a terrible birth, and she lay quiet at last under the thud thud thud of his still and beating body, her hands beside her open and relaxed.

Twelve

Under the warm effusion of a February chinook sun, Judith and Mina leaned against the corral fence, absorbed and intent. Judith's coat was open to the warm air, and poised there, her body was hard and muscular but soft too, with a kind of relaxed response, a grace and ease that she had only just begun to realize.

In the barn the pigs snuffled and whoofed with the pleasure of sun on the snow. It penetrated the walls, soaked into their gleaming hides, into their very bones. Outside they could hear Marie Antoinette's squeals and smell the hot reek of the boar's excitement.

"Well, he's certainly active," Mina said.

"He's supposed to be, especially considering how much money he cost." Judith's hair was longer now, covering her ears but still ragged and gamin-like.

In the corral the boar rushed and frothed at Marie Antoinette, the clean lines of his good breeding complementing her pale hide and dainty feet.

"Are you going to name him?" Mina asked.

"I haven't thought about it yet. Maybe."

Mina laughed. "When he proves himself."

Over the thick layer of straw that covered the still-frozen ground of the corral, the two shuffled and quartered, her quick evasion feinting his unwieldly masculinity. Along her neck and flank he nuzzled, mad with the scent of her, his hindquarters stiffening in his over-eagerness to jump her. She edged away then sloughed her body around to face him, whoofing and grunting.

The two women watched intently. "She's making him work," Mina observed.

"Of course." Judith laughed. "He has to pay."

"It's crazy, the positions we let them put us in. Having just got rid of eleven babies, that sow is going to let him put his forelegs up on her and stick that thing in her cunt, and god knows whether she will get any joy out of it."

"Don't make me feel so guilty," Judith said. "She gets to lead him a dance for a while."

They watched the snuffle and snort of the two pigs, the indignant squeal of the sow when he nipped her, rooted against her.

"And after all," Judith looked up at the sun for a moment, "that's all he gets to do. Only limited usefulness."

The boar's heavy balls jiggled as he circled the sow, snuffing her from flank to snout.

Mina grinned. "Yeah, you're right."

Against the fence the sow hesitated, giving him just enough time to jump her before she twitched her body away and his forelegs fell to the ground again. Enraged, he rushed at her, squealing, and pawed himself up onto her; mounted then he thrust the length of his emerging red shaft at her suddenly twitching and eager cunt. Under the push of his weight she set her four legs against the ground, held him up and encouraged his advance with quick, high squeals. Beneath the onslaught of his heavy clumsiness she staggered but held herself braced and quivering, until he dropped to the ground, whoofing and snorting.

Outside the fence Mina and Judith started to clap. The boar turned startled orange eyes on them as if caught doing something foolish. Then blindly he turned again to Marie Antoinette but she whoofed and snarled at him. His necessity dispensed with, she wanted no more of him. And at that the two women clapped again.

"You tell him, Marie Antoinette," cried Mina. "You tell him." And together they laughed, those insane women, laughed at everything they could and as hard as they could as they danced about in the melting snow.

Epilogue

Judith thumped her hand on the counter. "Any mail for me?"

He didn't move but stared at her from under those bush-like eyebrows. Finally he spoke and his voice was old and rusty. "You the lady with all those pigs?"

"Yes," she said. "I am."

He stood there so stubborn and reproving that it flashed on her and irrepressibly she threw back her head and laughed in his face, loudly and unafraid, her shouting mirth rebounding off his sour face like a mismatched echo. In that instant she felt something snap, some high-tension wire spring into release.

"Well. Humphh."

She stopped laughing as suddenly as she had started. "I'd like my mail please." She said it deadly quiet.

"Yes, yes." He shuffled over to the General Delivery boxes and came back with a handful of letters. He held them on the counter and stared at her again. "You ought to get a box."

And then they were staring at each other over the counter, eye to eye, unwinking.

"What for?"

"You get enough mail," he stated querulously.

"So?"

He took a breath, still held on to her letters. "Well, you know General Delivery is for folks just passin' through who ain't plannin' on staying very long. Folks that lives here has a box."

She suddenly smiled at him. "Really? How much is it?"

"Just five dollars a year. You've been here for a while now. You're not plannin' on leavin', are you?"

Her smile broadened. "No, I guess not. I'll get a box. Five dollars." She pulled a bill out of her wallet and laid it on the counter.

He dug into a drawer behind him and produced a key. "There you are then. Number 30. It's Johnson's old box."

"Thank you." She picked up her letters and waited until he had gone to sit down at his desk behind the counter. Then she walked to the wall of boxes, opened hers, number 30. Yes, the key fit. She laid her letters inside, shut the little door, pulled out the key. Then she inserted the key in the lock again, opened the door and took out her letters. With the key and the letters in her hand she walked out to the parked half-ton.

Sitting in the truck, she rifled through them, stopped at the unexpected square, white envelope. Carefully she laid the other letters on the seat beside her and tore it open. After waiting so long the letter seemed unreal, almost intangible. But no, she could feel the texture of the heavy paper under her fingers.

Inside was a single sheet of paper, written in his tight, close handwriting. The lines blurred in front of her eyes and she leaned her head against the steering wheel. Damn. Without reading the letter, she put it back in the envelope and flung it on the dashboard, spun a furious U-turn in front of the post office, then drove home, gravel flying behind the speeding truck.

In the yard she slammed out of the half-ton and ran to the barn, flinging herself through the door like an animal into a cave, crying bitter and unrestrainedly as she stood there in the aisle, hanging onto the fence with one hand and knuckling at her face with the other.

For a long time she stood sobbing, then gradually grew quiet. Her head cocked to one side, she listened to the pigs shuffling and rooting in their straw. A perfect and murmuring silence hung in the air; their bodies glowed through the diffuse light. In the corral they could hear Marie Antoinette and the boar snuffing at each other. Judith walked up and down the aisle a few times, taking deep breaths, then stopped at the end of the barn. "Pigs," she said. "Pigs." And she opened herself for them, stretched herself wide and unending, her arms out, her head tall, her legs long.

"Pigs," she said, "you win."

ABOUT THE AUTHOR

Born in 1954 in Wetaskiwin, Alberta, ARITHA VAN HERK grew up on a farm near the village of Edberg, Alberta, and attended the University of Alberta, graduating with an Honours B.A. in English in 1976. In the same year she won the *Miss Chatelaine* short fiction contest for "The Road Out," which was subsequently published in that magazine. Her short fiction has also been published, among other places, in an anthology, *Getting Here*, edited by Rudy Wiebe. She received her M.A. in English, specializing in creative writing, from the University of Alberta in the summer of 1978. Ms. van Herk has worked at various times as a farm hand, tractor driver, secretary, researcher, teacher, editor and bush cook. She is currently writing full time, living in Edmonton with her husband, geologist Robert Sharp.